FIFTY-TWO STITCHES

HORROR STORIES

FIFTY-TWO STITCHES

HORROR STORIES

edited by Aaron Polson

S

Strange Publications
Lawrence, Kansas
www.strangepublications.com

A STRANGE PUBLICATIONS book
published by arrangement with the authors

First Edition: December, 2010
All Rights Reserved

ISBN-13: 9780982026656

Cover art by Aaron Polson.

For Jamie Eyberg, a friend and fellow writer.
You are missed.

Contents

KILL YOUR DARLINGS

John Paolicelli, Jr.

He sat in the dark living room holding the letter close to his chest. Finally, after hours of procrastination, Eddy opened it. The note from the editor simply read: "My advice to you is to kill your darlings."

It wasn't the in-depth response he had hoped for. What was supposed to be constructive criticism somehow managed to piss Eddy off. He crumpled the page into a ball and muttered, "Kill your darlings."

He had heard it all before, but this rejection stung more than usual."Stock Broker Massacre" was his favorite story, and he expected a better reception for the shorter version. After so many professors and editors had critiqued his writing as wordy, he concentrated on being succinct, and thought he nailed it with this, the eighth rewrite.

Okay, let's clean this up one more time.

He tossed the manuscript onto his empty desk, pulled a file labeled "submittals" and a sharpie from a drawer, and placed them next to it. The rejection letters and writing projects from college once served as inspiration, but were now just painful reminders of his failures.

His dead eyes stared at the manuscript until the words blurred into gray haze. He shook his head, refocused, and then scribbled, "KILL YOUR DARLINGS" across the title page in giant letters. A sad laugh escaped as he exhaled.

He was introduced to the phrase by his first rejection letter. Eddy found it humorous, and had it printed on a t-shirt in jest. And though it wasn't funny anymore, he pulled the shirt from his dresser drawer and put it on.

Maybe this will change my luck.

He leafed through the file, searching for hope in the scrap pile. Among the form letters were a few personal notes of encouragement. But as he came to the last, "Kill your Darlings" again jumped from the page. He grunted.

He pulled out a story he wrote in college."While your attempts to cut out the fat are admirable, you still need to kill your darlings," was written neatly in red below the C+ in the right hand corner.

Cut out the fat. Kill your darlings.

He reread 'Stockbroker' again. A red pencil circled and scribbled until the pages were left bleeding. An hour of intense self debate ended deadlocked, and in the end, he left the piece as it was. He sighed.

He read it aloud. The words seemed to dance rhythmically from his mouth. He shook his head, and threw the script across the room. He sat motionless for a long while, glaring at the pages scattered over the carpet.

"Kill your darlings," he mumbled.

"Eddy it's six a.m. Why are you still up?" his roommate Jim asked on his way to the bathroom.

"Just doing some editing."

"Maybe someone should've edited that shirt. 'Darlings' is spelled wrong."

Eddy pulled the shirt away from his chest and glanced down. He shrugged his shoulders."It figures."

"Shouldn't you be getting ready for work? Wall Street waits for no one."

"No, got laid off last week. They blamed the economy."

After a pregnant pause, Jim changed the subject."Your story is good, but could be shorter. You need to visualize the story through the eyes of the killer. Get rid of the stuff that doesn't advance plot. Then go back and kill your darlings."

Kill your darlings.

Eddy nodded absently, his eyes fixed on the folder on his desk. Before he looked up, Jim had dressed, grabbed his gym bag, and hustled out.

"Through the eyes of the killer," Eddy whispered, as he trudged to his bedroom closet and grabbed his hunting rifle.

Through the eyes of the killer.

With the manuscript in one hand and the rifle in the other, Eddy went to the window and opened the shades. From his perch eight stories up, he watched the city awaken through the scope of his rifle.

Below, a pretty blonde waited for the bus. She fiddled with a BlackBerry, grinning as her fingers clicked away.

There's the ex-girlfriend. She really doesn't advance the plot.

Gotta kill your darlings.

Bang! The girl crumpled to the ground. A screaming man dove behind a dumpster, sending seagulls flying in every direction. Eddy watched through the scope with a satisfied grin.

Looks good.

He picked up the manuscript and wrote a few notes in the border, then turned his attention back to the street. A man in a dark suit came out of a doorway and strode toward the subway.

"Just doing some editing," he whispered as he moved the crosshairs onto the man's forehead.

PICTURE THIS

Anna Taborska

Picture this: you've been hanging around for years in Uncle Geoffrey's stinking dark house, waiting for the old codger to pop off so you can inherit his loot. You've wasted your youth listening to his plaintive gibbering and cleaning out his bedpan. Finally, you can't stand it anymore. You wait until he's asleep and then you put his pillow over his face and push down hard until he stops kicking. Then you dig a hole at the bottom of the garden and bury him in it. At last you're free to live your life the way you deserve.

But Uncle Geoffrey comes back. And he brings with him Aunt Mildred, cousin Hildegard and a dozen other decomposing occupants of the local cemetery. They shuffle grimly towards the house. You try the back way out, but are stopped by a rotting corpse with green guts dangling from its bloated belly. You bolt the doors and secure the windows, but from somewhere to your left you hear the sound of breaking glass.

Then the front door comes flying off its hinges, and enter Uncle Geoffrey, his face grey and his eyes still bulging from the strain of breathing mucus-covered pillow instead of air. He moves towards you stiffly, rigor mortis turning his fingers into talons and his legs into rigid planks of wood. He's drooling down the front of his gown, and his bloodshot eyes never blink. From the way he's staring at you, you can't tell if he's overcome with rage or if he just wants to rip your head off and eat your brains.

You fumble with the shells for the shotgun you've just wrenched from the cupboard in the corner. You aim at Uncle Geoffrey's head and pull the trigger. Uncle Geoffrey's head explodes. But Uncle Geoffrey just keeps coming...

THE SWEETEST CANDY

Joshua Rainey

Million Dollar Teeth smiled. His gold teeth shimmered in the buttery light. In his hand was another jar of honey and a Dixie cup with Albert's vitamins. Albert's diet consisted solely of honey for the past two months. He vomited the sweet substance, he shit the sweet substance, and he dreamed about the sickening sweet substance.

"*Mjaltë Më shumë për ju njeri sheqeros.*" The huge olive skinned man laughed. Albert didn't understand a word that had been spoken to him since he had been taken captive. Nor did Albert know why he had been captured.

Another man appeared in the doorway, Babyneck, he was an immensely fat man with an undulating neck like a baby huddled under his chin. "*Si është gjë e ëmbël tona sot?*" At that both men laughed.

Million Dollar Teeth set the jar down on the stone floor, and both of Albert's captors left the room. Albert heard the door being locked and screamed. "What do you want from me goddammit! Tell me! Someone speak fucking English!" Albert's voice grew hoarse, and tears streaked his hollowed cheeks.

In the background Albert could hear a buzzing drone that never stopped. It was the bees. They never slept. Albert never slept.

Albert paced his chamber and stared at the amber liquid in the canning jar. They knew that eventually the gaunt American would eat the honey. He always did, it was just a matter of waiting. Albert stared down at his forearms. They were frail. His frame was dwindling. His teeth were loosening. Albert was probably losing his mind.

"*Hani, ju do të jeni nevojë për fuqinë tuaj.*" Albert heard Million Dollar Teeth laugh outside his door. Every night he could hear him and his friends, Baby Neck, and

9

MGD playing cards and drinking.

The only light Albert had came from the other side of the glass window of his chamber, and it shone in through a wall of honey jars casting him in amber.

The bees never slept.

Hungry, Albert grabbed the jar, and tore off the lid. He reached his curled fingers inside to scoop out the contents. The honey drooled down Albert's chin, and snarled in his chest hair. Albert scooped the liquid into his mouth greedily. Beads of honey had hardened in his hair, and the length of his naked frame. After two months Albert no longer cared.

Albert knew that soon Million Dollar Teeth would leave him a glass of water under the door. Besides the honey, it was the only nourishment he was allowed.

Albert looked up from his gluttony, and saw his three captors tapping on the glass and laughing. All three were smoking long thin cigarettes.

"Ju duken aq i mirë sa mund të hani të gjithë ju lart." Babyneck chuckled. Albert smiled at the fat man's neck. He thought that it had to be a growth of some sort.

As quickly as Albert ate the honey it came up in a gut-wrenching wretch. Then everything went black.

Albert slept fitfully. The droning of the bees kept creeping into his mind. When he did awaken Million Dollar Teeth loomed above him. Albert was shackled, hands and feet.

Million Dollar Teeth waved for Albert to stand up.

"Sot është ditë e madhe." He smiled.

Albert stood on shaky legs. Obediently he followed Million Dollar Teeth out of the room, and down a long earthen corridor lit with bare bulbs hung on chains. Million Dollar Teeth whistled a solemn tune that made Albert's skin crawl.

"Ah, here we are." The bastard smiled at the trembling American.

They were in a large sparsely furnished room whose only distinguishing piece of furniture was a large rectangular box. The box was a sturdy, clear, plastic box that frightened Albert. Next to the box was an open earthen hole.

"You sonuvabitch," Albert cried. Tears stained his emaciated cheeks.

"What? You don't like your new accommodations?" Million Dollar Teeth asked. His voice was cocky and smooth. Albert wanted to punch him, but it took an effort just to remain standing. A part of Albert was relieved just to hear English again.

Albert stared at the box. "No." He understood this to be his new accommodation, and nearly collapsed. "No!" MGD and Babyneck grabbed Albert by his arms and held him.

"Yes. You see you are going to be a confection of sorts. You are going to be placed in that coffin which we will fill with honey, and in a few years you will be dug up and fed to the rich as a holistic medicine." Albert struggled to break free but they were too strong for him.

"Goodnight," MGD said before Albert felt a prick in his arm.

THE RISE OF AZALIEL AND LORCAS
Michael Stone

I perch on a rock rimed with frost and gaze at the distant horizon. When my brother Lorcas and I became stranded during a routine reconnaissance of Hell, we'd expected God's forces to mount a swift rescue operation—and been disappointed when none came.

And so, as the days wore on, we had squatted inside the *Bottle*—a brass cylinder mounted on cartwheels and powered by holy fire—and braced ourselves to have our squashy bits stamped into the earth by the legions of demons waiting impatiently outside. Instead, when the warding prayers finally expired and we were dragged through the aft porthole, the hordes had simply roughed us up a bit: a bite here, a gouge there, and lot of farting in our general direction. Positively a welcome by demon standards. Probably because we'd looked nothing like angels by then; the presence of sin had corrupted our immortal forms.

The frost makes my tail itch. I scratch it as I stare at the mile-high wall cutting me off from Heaven.

"Forget it," a voice grates near my ear. "You're not going back."

I turn on my rock to face the speaker. "Don't bet on it, you spiky-faced—oh! Sorry, Lorcas, I—I didn't recognise you with the, um..." I avert my gaze. Lorcas had been such a beautiful angel with his rosebud lips, baby blue eyes and blond curls. Four days in Hell and his face looks like a porcupine is copulating with it.

Copulating. I shake my head. I shouldn't even know words like that. The presence of sin has corrupted us spiritually as well as bodily. I go back to contemplating the far-off wall.

"They'll come for us," I say, stubbornly

Lorcas tips his head to the milling demons. "Face it, Azaliel, we are just like them now."

12

I regard our bodies with sadness. The black scaly skin, stunted wings and the inchoate horns prove his point, and the thing that meets my eyes when I peek under my loincloth isn't something an angel should be packing either. Lorcas, sadly, has been exploring new avenues with his beastly equipment. He even tried to have his wicked way with me. Only a swift prayer and an even swifter raised kneecap deterred him from exploring *my* avenue.

"But I don't *feel* demonic, Lorcas. I miss life in the Celestial City. I miss—wait, what's that?" I point to a star in the blood-red sky. It descends and the blurry light concentrates into a golden disc. Only one caste of the nine choirs possesses a non-humanoid form.

Lorcas gasps. "It's a throne!"

"Quick, Lorcas, to the *Bottle*!"

I run and dive through a porthole. The vessel creaks as the throne exerts its influence, and then lifts gently off the ground. Several demons try to follow. I thrust the stowaways out.

Lorcas is still standing where I left him.

The *Bottle* is gaining height.

"Lorcas! Quickly, before it's too late!"

He shakes his head slowly, as one resigned to his fate, then runs and makes a desperate leap. I grab his wrists and haul him inside.

"For a horrible moment there I thought you'd decided to stay."

The quills on his face wobble as he smiles. "It was something you said, about missing the Celestial City."

"Yes, it will be good to get back to the choral singing, the mission briefings, the camaraderie..." I trail off when I realise that his smile is a bitter one. "What is it?"

"You think they'll welcome us back when they see us like this?"

I had no answer, for I had given no thought to what sort of homecoming two corrupted angels would receive. Not a pleasant one, I suppose.

"Then why *are* you coming back, Lorcas?"

"Because someone missed his welding classes."

"What?"

He gestures to the battered *Bottle* with a talon. "Sin got in and touched us because someone screwed up the welds. We never stood a chance."

"The cherubim do the welding."

His coal-red eyes narrow to slits. "I know."

We kick out a side panel as we pass over mile-high gates. Overhead, the throne hums a rousing hymn, while far below verdant fields form a pastoral quilt, pierced here and there by pearlescent minarets. There is an uneasy feeling in my throat. I think it is anger or resentment, or something equally foreign.

Lorcas follows my gaze, and the spines on his face rearrange themselves into a malevolent grin. "What say we go kick some cherubic ass, Azaliel?"

I try to hold back the words on my tongue, before succumbing to the uneven struggle.

"Fucking A, brother."

*Author's note: Azaliel assumed the throne was humming a hymn. It was actually Wagner's "Ride of the Valkyries".

BLUE PLATE SPECIAL
Nick Contor

The operating room was dim, but Javier preferred it that way. He could see well enough as he placed the medical equipment in the spot assigned to it. The doctors and nurses at Presbyterian Hospital (heck, any hospital) were very particular about the positioning of equipment. Seconds were often crucial in the OR, and no one wanted to tell Mrs. McKenzie that her husband had passed away suddenly but couldn't be revived because the defibrillator had been put away in the wrong spot.

Javier was in charge of OR cleanups because he was careful. Every box of gauze, every scalpel, every monitor was back in the proper place when he was done. He had been working at Pres for ten years now, and liked it much better than his previous job at Our Lady of Mercy. Too many priests and nuns around there, all of them decked out in their work clothes.

Presbyterian was much more ecumenical. You could walk through the halls here at Pres for years and not see anything resembling a religious artifact.

Javier had righted a fallen tray table and was about to go out to the hallway to fetch his mop and bucket when he saw the small blue basin, seemingly tossed carelessly in the corner. It must have fallen off of the table. Maybe the tray had been knocked over by a nurse in a hurry, or a tech carrying the patient out following surgery. The circumstances were unimportant, the tray was what mattered.

It lay forgotten, inside was a medium-sized puddle of blood. Some of the blood had splashed up the side of the basin, and a few drops were splattered on the wall, but Javier ignored them. His interest was in the basin, which had retained almost all of the blood.

He licked his lips.

These were the times he waited for. The reason he was working here. He knew the Hazmat procedures backwards and forwards, knew about the proper disposal of biohazardous material. And no one ever complained about Javier's work. The OR was always left spotless when he was finished with it.

He slowly lifted the basin. It was a relic from years past. Blue porcelain containing rich, red blood.

His lips parted to allow his tongue to snake out, slowly running along the rim to catch the splatters, which were not even dried yet. He tipped the basin, watching with anticipation as the blood flowed ever so slowly towards him. Just slightly congealed. Perfect!

His eyes closed as the blood flowed over the edge. His Adam's apple bobbed and a low moan escaped. He swallowed until the flow slowed, then tipped the basin further to lick along the inside surface until the blue porcelain gleamed with his saliva. He quickly examined the bowl to be certain he had not missed a drop before depositing it along with the other pieces destined for sterilization.

The few droplets on the wall were quickly taken care of with a bleach-soaked rag. Javier had already taken quite a risk by feeding out in the open. He would have a tough time keeping his job if someone happened to walk by the OR and saw an orderly licking the walls. Very difficult to explain that one.

Javier smiled as he wheeled his cart outside to grab the mop and bucket. This was why he loved working in a hospital. He knew he would never starve.

SECOND SIGHT!

Kurt Newton

It ran like an unending torrent of hot molasses, like the seaweed green vomit extruding from little Regan's mouth in the Exorcist. Blood. So much of it. Too much of it, pouring from the old man's eyes.

"I can see... I can see... "

It was all the old man had been saying since he was brought in to the emergency room.

"Where was he found again?" said Doctor Marks, plastic face shield securely in place.

Nurse Penny pulled her eyes away from the twin rivers of blood long enough to comment. "In an alley behind St. Joseph's church. A nun heard him howling and called 911."

"Bet she thought it was stigmata." The doctor shined his penlight in the old man's eyes and flicked it to the side. "There doesn't seem to be any damage to the eyes themselves. The source of the bleeding appears to be anterior."

"But Doctor, if his brain were hemorrhaging, wouldn't it be exiting his ears, nose or mouth. Why just the eyes?"

"Some hemorrhaging can be more localized. It's rare with the brain, however." The doctor continued to hover over the old man, shining his penlight. "Strange... "

As Doctor Marks moved in for a closer inspection, the old man's body convulsed. Veined hands with gnarled fingers reached up for the light. "I can see... I can see..." the old man cried, his voice hoarse, his neck strained. The old man then collapsed, his breathing and the flow of his blood slowing to a stop.

"Should we call it? Doctor?"

Doctor Marks had turned away to avoid the old man's death-throe spasm. He turned back to Nurse Penny and the now deceased patient. "I'm sorry, nurse.

Yes...time of death—" Doctor Marks squinted at the clock on the wall. His vision momentarily blurred. "Four fourteen p.m."

He removed the face shield, snapped off his gloves and untied his gown, and tossed them into the trash. "Nurse, I'll be in the private lounge if anyone needs me."

For Doctor Marks, it felt like a headache was coming on. The hallway light hurt his eyes. The lounge was dark and empty. He went straight to the couch and stretched out.

Funny how, even though it was dark, he could see a strange illumination. The outline of the room glowed like a polarized picture. What was dark was light, and what was light—like the thin line underneath the room's entrance—was dark. Even with his eyes shut, he saw light, tiny streamers, as if he were looking into a microscope at the blood vessels in his eyelids. He got to his feet and walked to the bathroom, unsure of what was happening.

He flicked on the light and an explosion of stars filled his vision. The image in the mirror was hideous, nothing but veins and corpuscles and filarial wisps of moving fluid. In his eyes were twin upside-down crosses, death signs, burned into his retinas.

He wanted to scream but instead his mind replayed the incident with the emergency room patient—only from the old man's point of view. He saw himself hovering over him, the penlight shining like a beacon into his eyes. Then came the sudden convulsion, and a single drop of blood rose upward, arcing in slow motion in an unnatural trajectory, above the face shield, landing in his eye.

A sudden hunger gnawed at the doctor's gut and he doubled over in pain.

He shut off the light off and stumbled out of the lounge into the hallway. He needed to get back to the emergency room. Along the way he was assaulted by all manner of hideous replicas of human transformation:

goblin, devil and demon faces; some asked if he was all right.

But nothing was all right, nothing would ever be right again, unless...

He burst into the emergency room, avoiding the stares of ghastly maintenance men and grotesque nurses, and lurched over to where the old man had died. A plastic basin sat on the floor, the old man's blood still in it. He picked up the basin. In the blood he saw creatures swirling, amoeba-like, the substance of life. Before anyone could stop him he tipped the basin to his lips and gulped the thick liquid. The room spun and he collapsed.

A DELICATELY BEAUTIFUL HAUNTING

Mercedes M. Yardley

She reached out for his hand. It was natural. It was what they had always done.

He wrapped his bony fingers around her soft ones.

"Are you certain that you want to do this?" he asked her. His voice was strained.

He wanted to blame it on his decaying larynx, but that wasn't entirely it. He cleared his throat, tried again. The same tight, rough voice. "You know that you don't have to."

She didn't say anything for a long while, but stood perfectly still. Her pink toes were lined up neatly with the edge of the cliffs. Water rushed and roared beneath her bare feet.

"It's beautiful," she said.

The wind tossed her hair around her face and pulled at her clothes. It made a strange morose whistling through the holes in his cheeks. For a brief moment, he was deeply ashamed of his appearance, of what he had become. As if she knew what he was thinking, she tightened her grip on his hand.

"I'm glad that you came back," she said. "You don't know what it was like living without you."

Simple words simply said, but they touched what was left of his heart. He would have cried if he had been able to.

She looked at the sky. "I thought that it would get better, that I would forget you eventually. Isn't that what they always say?"

He studied her profile. Her eyes were sad, but nothing else had changed. He spoke softly.

"I don't know if I want you to do this. I don't think you understand what you're giving up."

She turned to him and smiled.

"I just want to be with you. It won't work with you being on my side, so I'll cross over to yours." She looked at the water and laughed. "I think that I'm a little scared."

He took both of her hands and pulled her to him.

"I'm with you. Just look at me. Think about something that will make you happy. Remember our first dance?"

Her eyes lit up. She remembered. She remembered and it was time.

He nodded his head slowly. "Keep thinking about that."

He had planned to nudge her but she surprised him. She took a deep breath and let herself fall.

The sound of the wind and water blurred together. He wrapped his arms tighter around her, protectively, as if he could somehow shield her delicate bones from the rocks and thrashing surf.

He couldn't, of course. That was the whole point. But he didn't know if he could listen to her fragile body break against the stones, or failing that, watch her gasp for breath under the waves. Would she cling to him? Would she scream his name? Would she push him away? All of these thoughts came so quickly, but they had only been falling for two seconds, maybe three.

"That song that you used to sing. The moon song. How do the lyrics go again? After you died, I couldn't remember them."

He was surprised but pleased. "The wolf comes from the forest and howls at—"

When it happened, it happened in silence. She made no sound, and his thoughts were swirling in the wolf-filled moon.

BY THE FIRELIGHT
K. Allen Wood

It had been a cold night, but I remember the heat most of all.

I sat across from the fire, Ashley by my side and nuzzled against my shoulder. She shivered uncontrollably. I put my arm around her, gave a reassuring squeeze and watched our breath crystallize and battle the heat pulsing before us.

We didn't roast marshmallows or tell ghost stories by the firelight; we didn't laugh, we sat in silence, thinking.

My thoughts traversed my bedroom, from corner to corner, floor to ceiling. I saw my guitar, video games, comics (and inevitably, tucked away between the covers of *Zombie Boy Rises Again*, the loose pages of *Playboy* I had pilfered from my father's old collection before he died). My baseball trophies shimmered and shined a golden orange as my mind's eye floated among my possessions. There were tears in that eye.

Ghosts emerged from the shadows, furtive and silent. Everything passed in a blur.

The fire was mesmerizing; it danced and swayed and hissed before my eyes like a deadly cobra caught by the hypnotic music of an Indian snake-charmer. Wood sizzled and popped and split wide, exposing fiery red veins.

Slowly, night pulled back its veil, and the ghosts brightened, stark, determined; they shouted and gestured wildly, like a spectator crowd waiting for the charmer's music to die, for that killing blow to finally come.

And it did come.

While I was mourning the loss of my precious things, Ashley was thinking about something else. She whispered, "I hope Mom's not in there."

And there it was: the killing blow. Finally come. So simple, so *expected.*

I was immediately ashamed, for being so selfish, for not opening my goddamn eyes. But our mother shouldn't have been in there, I protested; she should have been shopping.

Shopping!

"Call me when you get home. Dinner's in the fridge," she'd said from the kitchen doorway, as Ashley and I left for the movies. "I'll be home late tonight; going shopping with the girls."

But it wasn't late, and her car was there, in the driveway. Waiting, silent, bathed in that shimmering orange glow.

Like us.

Flames slithered both within and without our home like maggots devouring flesh. New sounds and lights assaulted me, the frantic voices of firefighters and police officers and curious onlookers rose and fell like violent ocean swells, and all at once the shutter of my mind opened wide, revealing a panoramic nightmare.

I closed my eyes and tried to will it all away.

It didn't work.

I tried again, and again, and again. It never worked.

I remember the heat most of all. It mocked. It spat. It stole. As I sat there, across from the fire, Ashley by my side, it burned.

IF YOU SEE A FISHERMAN, YOU BETTER LOOK AWAY

Deborah Walker

Alice pushed her mother around the park. It was a cold and blustery morning, a miserable day. A fine, dirty rain drenched them both. At one time, her mother would have called it 'mucky weather'. They came to the park every morning, come rain or shine. Alice needed to get out of the house.

Alice pushed the wheelchair into the Memorial Garden, where thieves had stripped the Memorial and sold the names of the war-dead for the price of scrap metal.

Alice saw the fisherman, dressed in scales that caught the light even in the feeble November sun, a man-shape with the face of an ocean beast. He stood immobile in his impenetrable armour, an unseen force-field which repelled all earthly weapons.

Alice stared at him, transfixed, as he turned his head, so slowly, as if moving through water. He returned her gaze with white-filmed, unblinking eyes.

Alice was caught. She was drowning in the star seascape of his old-eyed imagination. She washed clean in the unconceivable sights of his understandings.

The fisherman broke the connection. He walked past Alice and out of the gate.

Alice stood gasping in the Memorial Garden. She looked around. She was alone. Alice had heard stories of groups of concerned citizens who were prepared to take action, the vigilantes prepared to root out any alien taint.

"Alice," asked the thin voice of her mother. "Who was that? Was it the devil?" Mother was confused, sometimes.

"No, Mum. Remember, I told you about the fisher-men. They live here now. We can't get rid of them."

24

Alice crouched down to face her trembling mother. "Did he look at you, Mum? Did he do anything strange to you?"

"I don't know what you mean, Alice."

Alice pushed her mother home. Pretend that everything is normal. Pretend that you're still normal and everything will be fine.

Alice sat in the living room, thinking about everything she had heard about the fisherman. Fishermen copy your mind and upload your emotions. Alice shivered. She had felt the touch of his strange mind. Then they sell you. There's a thriving market for mind clones in the universe, apparently. Her life, her mind, which seemed so ordinary to Alice, would be considered an exotic, marketable commodity. Alice imagined herself copied into the body of some robot, insect, wave form, another species of life relishing her mind. There might be thousands of her mind clones, already.

The fisherman will copy and corrupt you. Her clone mind would be compelled to do new things. Who knows what strange desires might arise when merged in a new body?

What should she do? Should she join one of the self-help groups? Should she turn herself over to the government to assist their research? Alice shuddered.

No. Her first instinct was correct. She would carry on with her normal life, and wait. She wondered if anyone else felt like her.

"Alice," the familiar sound of her mother echoed through the house.

Alice walked to her mother's bedroom, "Mum, are you alright? You don't feel strange do you?"

"Is that devil coming again? He wants to steal your soul, Alice."

Alice thought how strange it was to imagine herself elsewhere, spinning through the universe in other bodies. She would sense a small part of her mind clones. They would send her psychic postcards though the immeasurable distances of space.

Everyone said it was a terrible thing to be copied and spun into a different body. It was the ultimate theft. The government was frantic. They could not rid the Earth of the fisherman.

We will become less than human.

"Don't worry mum," said Alice. She felt a twinge, and an image of an endless dark nebula entered her mind.

Alice smiled.

A fisherman had copied Alice's soul.

And she liked it.

EDIBLE FLOWERS PERCHED ABOVE A DYING LANDSCAPE

Cate Gardner

A square of paper marked with the blood seal lay across Moira's keyboard. With trembling fingers, she picked it up. Whispers stalked, following her along the corridor and waiting for the moment when she opened the note and read the words they already knew.

You're evicted. Only, the powers on high had worded it in a more eloquent, tied with a legal-bow manner. She ran her fingers across her wrists. She hoped they cut deep and fast.

Moira screwed the paper up and dropped it in the recycle bin. She blinked back tears and offered her colleagues a salute before marching out of the building. She understood their ghoulish behaviour stemmed a little from relief. Today it was not them.

One last deep breath and the change in air knocked her sideways, reminding that the world no longer turned for them. A distant grumble caused her to shudder.

A man holding a canister of oxygen and a mask picked her up off the pavement. She grabbed at his arm, pulled the plastic mask to her face and drew in long breaths.

"Easy," he said. "The air is thinner out here, but it will sustain you."

"Thank you," she said, despite his collaboration with the enemy.

He passed her a ticket marked 8A. "The ride from here to there is painless. In fact, you won't remember a thing." He meant to be kind. "It knocks for us all."

"I wish my blood poison," she said.

He backed away. No doubt, he'd heard the same line many times.

Regaining her composure, she watched similar scenes to her own unfold across the business district.

27

Around them, ghost faces peered out from the myriad windows in the surrounding glass towers. She knew by their distant gaze that they looked out towards the barren fields.

A soldier's life is worth that of a hundred citizens. The words scrawled in graffiti across streets not paved with gold. That epitaph she knew concealed the bold new truth—all the soldiers were dead and the law bowed to a new dictator.

The Revoking of Emancipation, Statute 101-B: Citizens have the right to eat, sleep and work in the towers until such time as the state requires the donation of their blood and organs.

What the wars had not killed, the new legislations would destroy.

"Line up, line up," a collector with a megaphone called from a bus numbered 8A. "See the hand of progression at work. You stand on the threshold of an exciting new future. Document your final thoughts and your words will be etched into history."

Or be deleted from it, Moira thought.

"Climb aboard. We will ensure your memory lives on in the Hall of Heroes."

Moira turned around, pulled her arm all the way back and hurled her briefcase at the collector. It hit him on the nose. She marched up to the bus and grabbed the megaphone from his startled fingers.

"Hear my words," she called to the evicted. "See your bosses choke on their vomit after drinking poisoned coffee. Watch a vacuum cleaner suck them up as if they were nothing more than a stale cornflake. Don't take this. Staple their butts to the desk and type them a letter of eviction."

The lack of applause shocked. "Have they snipped off your vocal chords? They murder us and you do not even whimper."

With the continued silence, Moira threw the megaphone aside and climbed aboard the bus. She pressed her hand down on the horn and released a primal scream. They had left her with no other choice. She started the bus engine, closed the doors, knocking the man off the step in the process, and revved the engine.

"Next stop, the end of the world," she shouted to the empty seats.

The avenue spun by in a dizzying stream of glass, metal and concrete. The convenience of living on a rock perched high above a ruined landscape meant it was a long way to fall. Tipping the vehicle over the edge, she crashed through the windscreen, somersaulted clear of the bus, and came to rest alongside all the other broken flowers that lay scattered in the dust.

With the final flickering of her eyelids, she saw her blood run deep into the cracked earth by means of a swollen tongue and knew it was not rocks that had split her skull but teeth.

A EULOGY FOR JIMMY
Uri Grey

I don't really know why I was chosen to give this eulogy. I mean, I'm not that great with words. People say I'm blunt and always say the wrong thing. And I guess a eulogy is probably the worst place to say the wrong thing. But what can I do? You ask and I deliver—I'm that kind of a guy.

So, Jimmy's dead. Obviously he's dead, or we wouldn't be burying him right now. I think he died from a drug overdose or something like that. I know many kids die from that shit these days, but I don't think any of them will be missed as much as Jimmy.

I know Jimmy touched us all in one way or another. I see now, how all the ladies cross their legs... yeah Jimmy sure loved his touching. Never asked for permission or even said "hello." Nope, he just went "Look! There's a bird," and wush, there's a hand down your... well never mind.

Jimmy loved many things, not only touching; he loved money, he loved horses, he loved fancy hats and shoes, he loved all sorts of words which I best not repeat right now. "Whatever he found, we lost" as the saying goes. I remember one time I caught Jimmy sneaking to my daughter's bedroom, so I slammed a pan right down his head and down he went on our carpet. I raised my pan again, you know how I am with kids... a bit hot-headed I guess, but my daughter woke up and said, the precious little thing, she said, "Dad, it's Jimmy, let him go." And I did. If she had the courage to say that and forgive him, then shame on me if I didn't!

I thought that thing would ruin Jimmy, but it only made him better. From that point, Jimmy really was an invaluable member of our small community. If there was some vice the little fiend didn't practice then it's only because I smashed it right out of his brains with that pan of mine. Otherwise, he was the very catalogue of evil.

Of course, a blessing like Jimmy can't last for long. "If you stray too far from God you're bound to fall someday." These are Father Habakkuk's words, not mine. So, I guess just to be contrary, Jimmy mixed alcohol, drugs, sex and whatnot one night and now he's with Satan now and we're left here crying for our loss. And I'm telling you, that's one big loss!

I mean, as long as Jimmy was here, his sins screamed so loud it made all of us look like saints. Salvation was ours! Sure, I roll the dice now and again. And you, Jeremiah, it's no secret you like sleeping late on Sundays. And, Miriam, I know you like to gossip here and there, eh?

Well, no more. Now that Jimmy's gone, we can't afford to be anything less than perfect. "You can miss a candle by the sun but not a candle by another candle." These are Father's Habakkuk's words, not mine. I'm not that great with words.

THE SLOUGH
Kent Alyn

The slough was as murky as Dave's belief in humanity.

In winter, when the brown water was deep, Safeway bags and toilet paper dangled from the briars; in summer, when dried hard like concrete, the place was a junkyard of beer cans, rusty appliances, and cat skeletons. The water was home to larvae, frogs, salamanders, and snakes; the muddy bank was home to skunks, possums, raccoons, and rats. Only nasty critters lived in the ugly slough.

Dave Franks hated the slough, though the waters called; if not the slough calling—the boy: Matty, the kid with the oversized hat and tight sweatpants that always waited for his mom after T-ball practice. After the last game ended, after the last hot dog sold, after the last car left, he sat against the cinderblock restrooms, hoping the next, or the next, or the next approaching car was his ride.

Three years later, Matty was forgotten, erased. The "Breaking News" moved on. The police did, too. Judging the way parents left their kids—waiting alone the way Matty waited—it was obvious the town forgot. Matty's mom, Donna, did. She moved to Colorado with her newest boyfriend, Methhead Hank.

Dave, a detective at the time, found Matty's Ken Griffey Jr. glove in the slough—nothing else. When the police gave up, Dave quit the force in protest.

Dave had no steady paycheck, no self-control, and no self-esteem, so his wife filed for divorce.

Finding Matty was all that was left.

Early spring, the slough was still deep enough to paddle. Dave hunted the slough on and off, usually alone. Equipped with a half-rack of Pabst he conned Pete Sanders into coming along, not so much to paddle, but to offer a second pair of eyes. The last time, Dave saw something unexplainable.

The baseball glove was at his feet, beside the camcorder and the beer.

"Damn no-see-ums," Dave said, slapping his arm.

"Stinks out here," Pete said, and then tossed an empty can into the water. "What's another can, anyway?"

Dave shook his head. That summed up Pete—didn't care much.

Pete stuck out his tongue and panted. "How much further?"

"Not much."

The stars and moon were out. Frogs croaked. A bat dove and touched the water. The raft cut through the ripple.

"Okay," Dave whispered, grabbing a low-hanging limb to stop the raft. "Over there, Pete."

The spotlight shone on the cock-eyed, clothes dryer across the slough.

"Last week I was right here when I heard a voice, saying words I couldn't understand."

"Bullshit."

"I ain't shittin' you. My neck hairs stood up. And then, I looked over at that dryer and saw a face, inside that dryer. Bulging, wide eyes, sharp cheek bones, and black teeth. It looked at me and then slithered out like an otter into the slough. The body—naked, yellowish—and the spine like row of rough knots. It went under and never came up."

Pete downed his beer. "What the hell?"

"Do you want to paddle over to there?"

"That thing live inside?"

He shrugged.

"Hell-no."

"You rather wait on the bank or come?"

Pete looked at the dryer, then at Dave. "Shit, I ain't stayin' here alone."

"Okay, let's keep it quiet," Dave said, and then handed Pete the camcorder. "Know how to use one of these?"

Closer, they paddled and then drifted, paddled and drifted. Dave kept the spotlight on the machine. Pete recorded.

They coasted. Grass stuck out of the open dryer. Something pale jostled. A hand crawled out.

Then, the creature looked into the light. A dead rat fell from its mouth.

Pete screamed as the creature climbed out and scurried behind the machine.

Dave shushed him, turning to see Pete ready to swing an oar.

A heavy rock sailed through the darkness, splitting a bloody gash in Pete's forehead. The big man teetered, and then splashed into the slough.

Dave hurried to the rear, the spotlight aiming up at the stars. "Pete!"

The raft rocked over the waves. He couldn't see. Turning to get the light, he saw the creature crouching at the front of the raft—the light angling upward at sinister eyes."

Dave surrendered his hands. He squinted and his eyes blurred. "I'll be damned, it is you. Just wanted to bring you something."

The creature's head tilted.

"There, buddy, by your feet. Ken Griffey Jr."

Matty picked up the glove, looked at Dave, and then leapt from the boat, escaping into the darkness.

A tear slid down his cheek. *Lost.*

RED SHOES

Danielle Ferries

Mia Millington watched from her position on the highest branch of the tree as a new friend arrived. The girl didn't yet wear the uniform but she'd look pretty in it. Like most new people she had a funny smile on her face like she was super excited about something but couldn't quite remember what it was. Her lips were smeared with bright red lipstick and her curly hair sprung around her face like a giant ball of orange twine.

Mia climbed down the tree slowly so as not to scratch her legs like she had the other day. Dr. Scott was cutting across the grass towards her and she wanted to talk to him before she went to meet her new friend. Dr. Scott was in love with her and it was only a matter of time before he asked her to marry him. Then she could live at his house.

She reached the bottom and twirled for him, hoping he'd notice her dress.

"Mia, I need you to come with me," he said, drumming his fingers against his clipboard. "We've found something in your room that we need to talk to you about."

"Okay." Mia batted her eyelashes exactly how she knew men liked. She was careful to walk two steps behind Dr. Scott because he didn't like it when she ran ahead, and she didn't want him to give her the shocks again. It burned and hurt like holy hell. She had to be good for Dr. Scott or he wouldn't want to marry her.

When they reached her room, Mia hovered shyly in the doorway. Dr. Scott didn't come to her room very often so she wondered if he was going to give her a special present.

"Come in, Mia."

She smiled and skipped across the room, wishing she had a skirt that swished. Her mother had once made her a pink one with frills.

"I want you to tell me what happened to Sally."

"Sally?" Mia asked as she studied herself and Dr. Scott in the mirror. She was a bit taller than him and wondered if it was bad for a wife to be taller than her husband.

"Over here." He motioned for her to come closer. "Don't be shy."

Mia turned and took four steps, her eyes resting on Sally's cherry red shoes. Her red shoes.

"What happened to Sally?" Dr. Scott asked again.

"She wouldn't play with me." Mia glared at the brown-haired woman.

"What game were you trying to play?"

"I wanted to play Dorothy and Toto, but I wanted to be Dorothy and she wouldn't give me her red shoes."

"What happened then?"

"She was mean to me. She said I was too ugly for pretty shoes." Mia nudged Sally with her foot and waited for a response. When she didn't get one she knelt down and pulled her hair. It made no difference and Mia straightened up and clapped her hands. "She can be my new dolly," she beamed. Sally was pretty enough to be her dolly, even though she wouldn't give back the shoes. And evil Nurse Mavis had taken her old dolly away so she'd had nothing to play with for weeks.

"Mia, Sally is dead."

"She's just pretending so she doesn't have to give me her shoes." Mia practised tapping her heels together, just like Dorothy had in the movie.

"Why is her corpse under your bed? What did you do to her?"

"Corpse?"

"Yes, Mia. Sally's corpse. Tell me what you did to her?"

Mia glanced at Sally's body. So still. "What a pretty corpse." She curled her fingers around Dr. Scott's. "Can I have my shoes now?"

36

THE WORM EATERS

John Boden

Lawrence watched the rains from his station underneath the carport. The clouds had literally rumbled in from nowhere, great black bison lumbering across the rainbow plain of sky. They snorted thunder and spat lightning. The sky opened and let loose a rain of maggots and worms that covered the ground in a fine, wriggling blanket. Children and emaciated adults scrambled from beneath their shelters to clamor and grab as many handfuls as they could, stuffing plastic bags and shoe boxes with living stringy things.

Some shoved great, gray handfuls into their slobbering, lipless mouths as they gathered. They moaned in disturbing ecstasy as they ate and cavorted in the slithering mud. In the shadows of his hiding place, Lawrence sat and watched and picked at the black sores that decorated his skinny legs. He popped the scabs into his eager mouth like candy, and, with disgust, grimaced at the worm eaters.

DRIFTWOOD

Daniel LeMoal

Something is wrong at Crane's Beach. I know, because I've been living here and fishing The Lake all my life. If you walk a half-mile beyond the service road, you'll see a small trailer and a series of sheds. It looks like nothing, but it is my home.

It has been over two years since I started to notice the broken bones along the shoreline, cracked and as dry as driftwood. I've called Parks and Wildlife, Fisheries and even the police. They all tell me the same thing.

"This is floodland, J.P. Cows and all sorts of animals get washed away and end up in the lakes."

Since I was a boy, I have seen many things wash ashore here. I know the difference between an animal and a person.

"Thanks for the call. Next time we're out that way, we'll take a look for you. Okay?"

They never come. They figure that Crane's Beach is all rocks, no sand and no people. They are wrong. The odd family will come, looking to get away from the crowds at the sanded beaches. They put on old running shoes and brave the stones to go swimming. Sometimes they barbecue on the beach well into the evening. I have no family of my own, so when I hear them laughing and singing, it makes my heart glad. Even though they don't come often, they are always welcome. I try to keep the beach clean, collecting the broken bottles, rusted hooks and stray netting. But surely they see the bones. I can't keep up anymore. Crane's Beach never gets many repeat visitors these days.

One Saturday, as I'm fixing one of my motors on the dock, I see a new couple walking on the beach. They make a camp for their lawn chairs and walk towards The Lake. The man and woman both scream, as they all do when they make those first steps into the frigid water. It's a big lake that never warms up.

My dog Mahkwa suns himself and watches as I put the motor back together. When I'm finished, I look at him and smile. That's when I see his ears perk up; over the wind, I hear more yelling from the beach. I can hear panic in their voices.

Mahkwa is already running down the shoreline. In the water, I see the couple swimming towards a flailing set of arms. A child? Maybe. Whoever it is, they are drowning.

I jump into my fastest outboard boat. Mahkwa barks at me as I speed away from land, the boat skipping on the waves. Past the break, the couple is floating together now; as I kill the motor and drift towards them, I see that the water has turned a cloudy red.

The man is already dead. The woman still holds onto him, keeping them both afloat. Even though a piece of her neck is missing, she tries to speak.

"The girl," she says, as her eyes start to roll into the back of her head. I look further out and see a small child floating in the water, face down. It's hard to leave the woman behind, but I rev the motor and steer towards the girl. I use my net to pull her towards me; she weighs next to nothing. When I pull her into the boat, she is already cold. Her skin is scaly to the touch. I roll the girl over and her eyes open; her mouth is filled with needle-like teeth that should belong to a walleye.

I recoil but she's already bitten into my leg, tearing away a large chunk of muscle. I kick with my other leg and fall overboard. She stands in the boat, watching as I try to swim away. I don't get very far; I've lost too much blood already. From behind, I can hear her as she jumps into the water.

Not like this, not like this, I whisper to myself. But then I grow faint and realize that it won't be long before my bones are driftwood, just like all the others: being worn down by the tide until there is nothing but dust. Then, at last, Crane's Beach shall have its sand.

SWEPT AWAY

Brenton Tomlinson

His tongue flicked out and dragged across parched and cracked lips. He held a grease-stained hand above his eyes in an effort to decrease the never-ending glare of the crystal blue water. In the distance, a bank of black and grey clouds marked the tail of last night's storm. Water, water everywhere, and not a drop to drink.

The yacht was a mess with tangled lines littering a battered deck. The mast had disappeared before midnight, the distress beacon flashing from the top as it sank beneath the black waters. If rescue came it wouldn't be because they managed to track that cry for help which now sat at the bottom of the ocean god knows how many miles to the south.

Mary-Anne had disappeared overboard about an hour later, quietly slipping into the ocean's embrace. In truth she looked peaceful and glad to go. Talk of separation had always been unpleasant to her, a reality she couldn't face. News of a replacement and pending divorce papers had been too much.

The fight had been short, but every bit as violent as the storm. His own much vaunted mast of patience having broken long before the yacht's central pillar relinquished to nature's torment. The boat hook was too convenient an object not to use, and Mary-Anne should have learned by now when not to push. The look of surprise and fear, mixed with a touch of betrayal, on his ex-wife's face lingered in his mind's eye.

The storm had washed away his torment and ruined his boat, but it had scrubbed the deck clean of Mary-Anne's blood as well. It had been easy, a moment of rage, a flexing of his superior strength, and the barbed steel penetrated her body more easily than he ever had. It had been difficult to pull it back out, but the thought was quickly forgotten when he drove it back in. The rush had been better than sex.

Rescue would see him start a new life with Trisha. If not, then maybe being claimed by the tainted waters would be a form of nature's justice. He shrugged and returned to trying to fix the engine. He'd kill for something to drink.

A smile crept across his face as a warm feeling grew in his gut. Well, he'd kill again for something to quench his thirst. He gripped the brine encrusted wrench tightly as a bubbling laugh crept through him.

Somehow he'd survive, he had to. Trisha wouldn't understand any more than Mary-Anne had, but his new thirst had to be sated.

THE TROUBLE WITH GNOMES

Jamie Eyberg

The lilac had come into bloom so we slept with the window open, enjoying the fragrance as it filled our bedroom. It was through the open window that we heard them. They were small but sharp, not unlike the sound of ice cubes exploding in a water glass from across a room.

I got up to see what was going on, thinking, perhaps, that a spring shower was moving in and the drops of rain were falling on the leaves.

I saw instead the moon, full and high in the sky. It illuminated the first buds of the roses and the petunias that had yet to establish themselves. Still the popping continued and I peered into the night to see what was the source.

That was when I saw the gnomes. The ones she had bought in bulk from the garden center. I watched as they all began to move, trembling really, the small concrete bodies crackled and popped as they did.

It was slight at first, then the rock facade crumbled and the gnomes moved more freely until they were running about, ransacking the garden and taking joy in pulling the petals from the flowers one by one. They stomped them into the dirt as they walked on small hoof-like prints that cut through the hard soil.

I said nothing but felt my wife come up beside me. We watched as they upended the fairy statue I had given her, the one with the bouquet of lilies in her arms, and buried it in the compost pile we had started the year before. The leftovers from the night before were still fresh on top and even in the dull light of the moon I could see rotting potatoes and eggshells.

We gasped as they took a brick that edged the walk path and threw it. It smashed into the fairy and shattered her into a thousand bits of ceramic and dust.

They laughed a coarse laugh as we watched it disintegrate. I couldn't help but notice that some of them were eying the birdbath in a most conspicuous manner.

It was the gasp that got us. They must have heard it through the thin walls and the open window. They turned their attention from the broken fairy and the birdbath and looked at us.

Hundreds of little eyes looked at us with ill intent and fresh bricks, torn from the earth as they came our way.

The only thing in their way was the window.

We both eyed the door and I almost opened it when she grasped my arm and I realized it opened into the garden. The first brick hit the window and a crack spirals across the glass.

DANGEROUS PREMONITIONS

Laura Eno

The first snowfall of the season dusted the ground in light powder, revealing small footprints that led to the cellar door. Jack shook his head in disbelief. What child would be wandering out here barefoot in the cold?

He scouted the area, not finding any other evidence before reluctantly coming back to the cellar, a place he'd avoided since moving in last month. One look into its dark, dank hold had been enough to dissuade him from further exploration. Who knew what lurked down there? Jack hadn't been keen to find out.

Returning from the house with a flashlight, Jack swung the wooden door open and peered inside. The musty smell of damp earth assaulted him, whatever traces of potatoes or onions it might have once held no longer discernible. He shuddered at the thought of black widow spiders hunkered down to spend the winter in cozy comfort.

The light played across the small space, showing a fresh mound of disturbed earth in the center of the floor. Thoughts of spiders faded as a small hand pushed up through the dirt, tiny fingers curling once before hanging limp.

Jack bounded down the rickety stairs, tripping and landing in a heap in his rush. He dug furiously, having only his hands for tools. His skin cracked and bled from the effort. Within minutes, he'd unearthed a small girl, no more than three or four years old. Her blue eyes stared forever fixed at a point beyond his understanding. Her mouth had been filled with dirt as if buried alive. All she wore was a tiny pink nightgown.

Gagging, Jack retreated back up the stairs and into the house. He called the police to report his findings. When they arrived, they found nothing amiss: no body, no small footprints, no soft dirt. Although naturally suspicious of Jack's story, there were no reports of a missing child. They labeled him a crank and warned him about making false calls.

Did he hallucinate the whole ordeal? Only his bloody hands told him no. When the footprints appeared again two days later with the next snowfall, Jack moved out, deciding the place was haunted.

One month later, three-year-old Abbie Tinsdale was reported missing by her mother, taken from the house sometime during the night. She mentioned the girl was wearing a pink nightgown. The police remembered Jack's report and checked the root cellar of the house where he used to live. They found the girl too late. She'd been buried alive.

The police arrested Jack based on his detailed description of the crime scene, even though he'd reported it a month before it happened, and the DNA evidence. His blood was mixed in the soil where the girl was found. They were convinced that only the killer would know such details, even accused Jack of setting up an elaborate alibi for himself with his story. The small town jury placed their trust in the hands of the law, sentencing him to life for a murder he didn't commit—but had the misfortune to predict.

THOR'S HAMMER

Alan W. Davidson

The three children floated on their raft in Diablo's pond. Meaghan, usually boisterous, was quiet today. Her knees were drawn up to her chest and she stared into the murky water.

Luthor nudged her with his shoulder. "What's wrong?"

She shrugged in response.

"Holy crap! Did you see that trout jump?" Dickie shouted.

"Shut up, I'm talking to Megs," Luthor shouted, swatting him with a rolled up horror magazine.

"Jeez, sor-ree!"

"We're your friends, right?" Luthor continued. Meaghan stared ahead, nodding slightly. "Tell us. Maybe we can help."

"It's just...I'd really miss you guys if we moved." she said.

"But you told us your mom wouldn't move again until you finished school. That's still four years away," Dickie said.

"Yeah...," Meaghan answered, tears tracked down her pale cheeks.

"...it's really got to do with that man—"

"What man?" Luthor said.

"You've seen him around. That creepy, bald guy at the end of Cochrane Street?"

"I know him. He hardly ever goes out."

"I've seen him too. He jogs every day. Just before dark," Dickie added.

"Tell us...," Luthor whispered.

"He's talked rude to me. Dirty stuff. He also touched me...," she added, glancing at Luthor through reddened eyes.

Luthor grasped the edge of the raft, his knuckles white. "Did you tell your mom?"

46

"She wouldn't do nothing. The same thing happened in Jersey three years ago."

"What did she say then?" Dickie asked.

"She told me it was all a misunderstanding. A week later she had us packed and moved here."

"I know you're worried," Luthor said. "But this is wrong and we're going to fix it." Dickie nodded in agreement.

"How?"

"Don't you worry about it, Megs."

The boys had found a large, moss-covered boulder on a hillside far from the path. Luthor's grandpa called it an erratic and said they were scattered all over New Hampshire during the last ice age. For three days they removed dirt from beneath the rock, propping it up with long bits of wood wedged into the dark soil.

On the Friday evening before Labor Day, Luthor stayed in the woods while Dickie waited near the jogging trail. As the bald man neared, the boy, frantically waving his arms, jumped into his path.

"Please help, mister—my friend's hurt!"

"What happened?"

"I think he broke his leg. Come quick!" Dickie said, and dashed through the trees. The man hesitated for a moment and then followed the boy. They ran far into the woods, eventually stopping at the boulder.

Dickie was breathless. "Down there, mister," he said, pointing under the erratic.

The man bent over the moaning boy. "Are you hurt?"

Dickie snatched the hammer that lay against the base of the rock and struck the man in the temple. Luthor scampered from the hole as his friend swung again, sinking the claw into the base of the man's skull. He screamed, clutching at the hammer as Dickie shoved him into the void.

Luthor grabbed a shovel and rammed the blade into the man's throat, unleashing a gush of blood. "That's for Meaghan, you perv!" he hissed.

The boys removed the wooden supports, causing the boulder to list forward. They shoveled the excess dirt around the edges of the rock and covered the soil with moss, leaves and branches.

Luthor watched the grey clouds from his office; the rain pelted the window and wound down the glass in sparkling tears.

The intercom voice startled him. "Dr. Guttormson, your patient is in exam two."

Luthor strode down the sterile hall, rapped the door and entered the exam room. A thin, vaguely familiar woman sat on the bench. She smiled and offered her hand. "I'm Meaghan King. You probably don't remember me, but my name was Murphy when we were in junior high."

Luthor chuckled and squeezed her hand. "Of course I remember you, Megs. How did you end up in sunny Seattle?"

"I'm in computer sales and my work transferred me here. Dickie Stein said I should look you up."

"Dickie? We haven't talked in years. When did you see him?"

"Years ago, after we moved back to New Hampshire. He showed up at my door one day selling life insurance. What a grand chat we had."

"That's great," Luthor said. He swallowed and leaned closer to Meaghan. "Didn't you and your mom leave town because of that bald guy...on Cochrane Street?"

She thought for a moment and laughed. "Oh that! Mom got another job in Boston and moved us away. Practically overnight. What I told you guys was a huge pile of crap. He never touched me—he never even talked to me."

LOCK AND KEY
L.R. Bonehill

I found the box on the day Richie Norton saved my life. I was just about lost to it; that sense of serenity that comes when you're drowning, despite your body thrashing as it struggles against the end. I was ready to let it all slip away, to fade into silence when Richie dragged me up from the muck and grime of the water and pulled me away to the embankment. I've never forgiven him.

We both lay panting and exhausted on the damp grass. Cold shivers ran through us despite the heat of the afternoon sun. Brackish water stung my throat and my lungs burned as they clutched for air.

Richie's yellow Spiderman t-shirt clung so tight I could see the rack of his ribs. The shirt was covered with algae and there was a ragged tear where it must have snagged on something in the water. He peeled it away from his chest and stuck his finger through the hole.

'You ruined my best shirt,' he said, scrabbling to his knees. He spat on the ground and ran a hand across his mouth, long fingers pulling at something on his tongue that wouldn't quite come away. He spat again.

'The hell you think you were doing?' There was a venom in his voice that was rare to hear from Richie. His eyes narrowed and he shook his head. 'Hope it was worth it.' He nodded at the box that I still held in one hand.

To this day, I don't know why I'd reached out for the box as it bobbed on the surface of the water, or how I'd managed to stumble in after it, or why I'd held it so firmly and wouldn't let go even as the life began to seep away from me.

I looked down and saw my knuckles were white, pale as the cataracts that clouded Grandma's vision.

The box wasn't much to look at; about the size of a hip flask from an old film noir, dented and battered all over, rusted clasps at the sides and a scuffed lock at the front.

'At least take a look inside, since you almost killed the two of us,' Richie said.

I flicked at the clasps, each in turn, and found they wouldn't budge. It felt light; I shook it and nothing seemed to move inside.

Richie snatched it away from me and dug his penknife out of his jeans pocket. It was the same knife his brother had used to carve three dots into his hand the year before. He'd promised he'd ink Richie with a crazy life tattoo just like it when he was older. Richie couldn't wait.

He prised the clasps apart with the blade and quickly moved on to the lock. It seemed the knife would give before the lock did. I could see the strain on his face, the tension in his muscles.

'That's not meant to be opened, no way,' he said and tossed the box back to me. 'You should be dead, man, you should be gone. Your eyes were rolled way up.' He mimicked the look and I shuddered as I saw the whites of his eyes.

He pointed at the box with his knife. 'You look after that, keep it safe; your soul's in there. Vida loca, my friend.'

Richie Norton was my best friend. Richie Norton saved my life. I never saw him again.

At school the next day Mrs Walker told us about the accident. Richie slipped in the bathroom and fell back into the tub unconscious. He drowned as the bathwater bled away.

Crazy fucking life.

I'm cold all the time now; it's as if the water saturated my bones. My palms and the tips of my fingers are still pale and wrinkled and there's a sour, stagnant taste in my mouth. Some days my lips are blue as the veins on the back of my hand.

There are times I'm sure Richie was just the first; the first of many. That everyone I've ever lost is because of that damn box, because I didn't die that day, because Richie was right.

Wait long enough though and answers always come. I found a key today, deep down in the mud by the embankment. It's small and the colour of dried blood and it's a perfect fit.

All I have to do is find the courage to turn it.

FOREPLAY

J. J. Steinfeld

During his retirement party, the math teacher was talking to the attractive science teacher, and she told him about her dream of having sex with an adorable visitor from a recently discovered planet. Drink in hand, he told her that two days after a Saturday double-feature matinee, enthralled by The Attack of the 50-Foot Woman and The Incredible Shrinking Man, he sat in elementary-school class and wondered aloud what would happen if the Amazing 50-Foot Woman went out on a date with the Incredible Shrinking Man but the teacher kicked him out as if he had drawn the Amazing Woman and the Incredible Man naked in his notebook, passing it on to every student in that long-ago class, completely warping their expectations of lovemaking for a lifetime to come. Then the science teacher, finishing her third drink, asked the math teacher, "If I were a sexy space alien, would you go to bed with me?" In his excitement, nostalgic film musings, and incipient drunkenness, the math teacher failed to notice the tiny tentacles that were emerging from the back of the science teacher's long, lovely neck.

THE MAN IN THE MIRROR

Samuel Montgomery-Blinn

My sleep had been dreamless, timeless blackness.

I don't remember waking up or how I got there, only squinting in the bathroom as the fluorescent tube blinked to life, flickering. I kept my tired eyes downcast, on the sink, my mouth feeling dry, like bones and ashes. I yawned and ran my fingers over my scalp, turned on the faucet, splashed icy water into my mouth and onto my face, swallowing and then letting the cold drops fall into the sink a while before toweling dry.

Suddenly I felt I was being watched and looked up to meet an unblinking stare.

My perfect, left-right reversed doppelganger looked back at me, mouth slightly open, breathing slowly, hands gripping the sides of the sink as he examined me like a stranger.

I found that I couldn't break his gaze.

Hypnotized, the man in the mirror used me like a puppet: preening, grinning, winking. Unconsciously I yawned and my eyes jammed shut, watering. I slowly cracked them open.

There he was, still locking my eyes with his stare. He looked tired.

"Good morning," he said without much enthusiasm, and I felt the same, crackled words escaping my lips. Standing straighter and smiling—I felt my spine jerk upright and my lips curl up in concert—he repeated the greeting, louder, more confident, as if to convince himself: "Good morning!"

When he finally frowned, sighed, and reached to turn off the light, my hand hit the frame and I realized the awful truth, a moment before returning to blackness:

I was the reflection.

BODY LANGUAGE
Jim Valenti

The warm sand and tropical breeze of Playa Tiburon was coaxing me to sleep when I heard the voice. It was calling to me in bulleted Spanish.

"El gran blanco devadora de hombres!" Huh? I squinted my sun-seared eyes upwards to find a black tussle-haired boy standing over me, pointing frantically down the beach.

"Rapidamente, por favor! Rapidamente!" he was sobbing.

I had been back in Cabo San Lucas barely an hour. After much too long of taking part in the ritualistic debauchery that is L.A. I had just up and left to kick back and take stock of my life. I felt the need to reacquaint myself with the ripping curls and virgin sands of my pre-corrupted surfer days and let time just take me where it may. The shimmering seas, lazy heat and cheap tequila of the Baja peninsula were the only tools I needed to start rebuilding. My possessions consisted of a pair of cut-offs, a long board and a frosty pitcher of margaritas. My brain and my Spanish were rusty, and I certainly wasn't interested in any interaction with the locals beyond a request for a "cerveza fria." But there he stood pointing excitedly down the strand and working himself into a panic.

"Gran blanco!" he repeated breathlessly, "Date prisa!" The beach was just about empty except for the two of us, and as my eyes started to regain focus I looked past his extended finger and saw the girl. She was maybe fourteen or fifteen, foundering in the deeper water just outside the surf break and a few yards down the beach.She was in obvious trouble, flailing wildly and beating on the surface in a frenzy to stay afloat. By the way she was panicking I knew she wouldn't last much longer. My indifference to the commotion going on around me washed away as my inner lifeguard rushed in, then instantly I was sprinting down the beach with the boy close behind. I charged headlong into the surf and came up in full swim.

I closed the gap swiftly and was on her in seconds. She was just slipping below the surface when I reached her and made a desperate lunge for her arms. They were flimsy in my grasp and I felt her strength slipping quickly away. I watched panic flash in her full, dark eyes—her mouth hung open in a silent scream as though she realized that death was upon her. Then she suddenly lunged forward and struck me above my eye with her forehead. Hey, I'm trying to save you here! I tried to stay afloat, although her body suddenly took on renewed life and began spasming violently all around me in the churning water. I went under briefly as she thrashed at my legs from beneath the surface. I pinned her arms back to get her under control, but they soon fell limp. She bobbed up and slipped beneath the water again. As she sank in a wake of colored foam her face finally relaxed and she uttered something that chilled my soul.

"Tiburon."

She wasn't drowning at all.

It's funny how quickly it all comes back. Playa Tiburon. I gasped for breath as I was pulled from below with renewed strength, this time not by the girl. Shark Beach. It was suddenly so familiar. Devedora de hombres—the man eater—the Cabo nickname for the great white. I felt my torso contort in grotesque rhythm, my new life of leisure all but assured as my legs were ripped one at a time from their sockets. I looked towards the shore where the boy stood crying and pointing. My margarita pitcher was tipped over and soaking slowly into the sand.

When I leave the institution I will return to Playa Tiburon, what's left of me, and console the boy. Instead of my long board I will pack a Spanish-English dictionary to go along with my new pair of cut-offs and my margaritas.

SOMETHING DIFFERENT!
Chris Reed

As Darren watched the obese woman get undressed, he wondered if he could really go through with this. Her breasts were enormous, which he didn't really mind, but the rest of her—the flabby arms, the double chin, the pouch of blubber that hung down over her crotch—had him second-guessing his decision to meet her here at the motel. After eight years of marriage, he'd grown accustomed to his wife's slim, athletic figure. She was the complete opposite of the woman who lay on the motel bed, sprawled out before him like a white, pasty whale. (He couldn't even remember her name. Was it Margaret? Margie?) Before he was married, Darren wouldn't be caught dead with a chick like this. She was a disgusting pig, so fat he couldn't see her genitalia. But he could smell it. Despite her obvious attempt to mask the stench with perfume, it still smelled like something had died down there.

But it was something different. So he took off his pants.

As Margo watched the man step out of his jeans and climb onto the bed, she felt her stomach growl. It had been a long time since she'd eaten, and this man was much thinner than she was used to—nearly anorexic—but she'd sought him out for precisely that reason.

As the man pushed her pouch up in search of her vagina, she delighted in the shock on his face when he saw her writhing nest of pubic hair. His eyes grew wide, jaw dropped, body trembled. He was so stunned he made no attempt to move as the wiry hairs reached out like insect feelers and coiled around his arms, wrists, legs and neck. He kicked and thrashed as they pulled him inside the gaping maw of her vagina. And when the teeth inside bit down on him, crushing those bony shoulders and knobby knees, ripping that long, lean torso in two, she felt oddly satisfied.

It wasn't the best meal she'd ever had, but at least it was something different.

THE NEIGHBOR

Dawn Allison

Emma Cannon was a stout woman with thick arms and a stern face, one of those sorts who like things best when they are precisely just so. She was dusting the windowsill when a rustling in the magnolia tree out front caught her eye. Damn squirrel probably into the birdfeeder again.

"Henry, get your twenty-two."

Henry glanced over his shoulder from his seat on the sofa. "What for?"

"Squirrel. Quick about it, now. Don't want him getting away." She scowled him into motion and while he was fetching the gun, she leaned on the sill, squinting out the window to find the vulgar little beast hiding behind the waxy leaves.

"Where?" Henry said, gun slung over his shoulder.

"Wait."

Henry waited. Generally, he was good at doing what he was told. That was why Emma loved him.

"Shit, Henry, I think you might need a bigger gun."

"Raccoon?"

"Ain't no coon up there, no sir."

"Well, what the hell, Emma, just spit it out already."

She shot an irritated glance over her shoulder, then turned her glare to the window. "It's that Jim Garby again, and damned if he ain't been pawing through our trash. Look at him, wearing that tablecloth I threw out three days ago."

Henry sighed. "I'll get the deer rifle," he said.

Henry was good at doing what he was told. That was why Emma loved him.

THE MANNERISMS OF RUNNERS

Barry Napier

It started off as an exercise thing, but now he has no idea why he runs. His leg muscles are toned and immune to shin splints; his ankles work like the hinges of a medieval drawbridge.

There is a rhythm to the wind against his face, to the pounding of his feet on asphalt like the heartbeat of a ghost. He runs and he runs and he has no idea where he is going. Three days ago he tasted salt in the air, the perspiration of the Pacific at his back. Today he smells manure and diesel. A large tractor trailer with a milk company logo barrels by like a big silver bullet looking for a werewolf that isn't there.

He has no idea why he is still running.

There are blisters on his feet and he is certain that both socks are filled with blood. He can feel the broken flaps of skin that were once the balls of his feet rubbing against the blood-soaked fabric. His eyes, lips and the insides of his nostrils are dry. His lungs are burning and there is the sensation of a weight that has sat upon his chest for so long that it has started to absorb into his skin, through his breastbone and into his heart.

Sometimes when the milk trucks go racing past, he thinks about jumping in front of one. Then maybe the running would stop and his muscles would get a rest in the ensuing explosion of calcium and Penzoil and New Balance.

He has been running for thirty weeks. He does not sleep. He only watches the world as it slumbers around him, clouds rising and falling and sprinkling stars like salt along the way. The night sky should represent rest, but it only urges him on. Run faster, it says. There is a maniac behind you.

Maybe that is why he runs; the maniac is surely still on his heels—the maniac he encountered on the corner

60

three blocks from his home. The maniac had worn a sheet of black that covered his entire body, standing outside a bakery at 5 a.m. among the smells of baking bread and dawn. He had looked like a shadow. The man had reached out and touched him.

Tripped him.

Joined him.

Is that why he runs?

Four days ago, he coughed out his tongue.

His calves are burning. The sun exchanges skies with the moon and another day begins. He keeps running. He tastes blood in the back of his mouth. His breath sounds like sandpaper dragging across shattered glass. A car passes and beeps its horn.

He raises his hand to wave and sees the decay on the underside of his forearm. There is no blood, only mottled gray splotches. It looks like mold on bread. This brings to mind the bakery and he peeks behind him to see if he is being followed.

The maniac is back there, gliding like a rogue shadow running from the sun. It runs without feet and points him onward. It then sinks into the road and leaves only the deserted Missouri highway (or was it Kansas or Connecticut or Calvary?) to show him where to go.

The laces of his shoes bounce up and down like the ears of a mauled rabbit. This scene looks familiar. He has been here before.

God, his feet hurt.

He coughs out his tongue; two days pass. A milk truck passes him, like a silver bullet looking for...

A car passes, beeps its horn.

He has run through this place before—always running, breathing electric pain, listening to the squishing sounds from his blistered feet in his soggy red socks.

He tastes the salt of the Pacific for several days. This is soon replaced by the wafting scent of manure and pastures.

He looks back and sees his companion, always pointing forward, always robed in black—a shadow cast not by light but by the absence of it.

He hears the approaching grumble of a milk truck as he brings his left foot up, right foot down, left foot up, right foot down...

He runs on and on.

Soon he will cough and his tongue will fall out. Then a car will pass, beeping its weak little horn.

He has been here before.

And no matter how hard he runs, he will never be faster than the shadow behind him or the truth it carries.

FIRE BOOMERS

Doug Murano

What a cluster-fuck, thought Officer Hammond as he crossed the threshold of the doorway into the machine shed. A drive out into the country to find an old man who'd worked himself to death in the July heat was one thing. But the smell coming in waves from inside the metal structure suggested a wild animal problem, and that was quite another thing entirely. He drew his pistol and moved forward.

Hammond couldn't call for backup. In a town the size of Cherry, he was the sheriff, the deputy, and the goddamn dog catcher. Besides, most of the town was already half-cocked at the Independence Day street dance. That meant yet another busy night, another holiday he'd have to miss.

The day's last light filtered through the small, rectangular windows spaced along the tin shed's long walls. Hammond's flashlight cut an alley of daylight through the spacious blackness that didn't reveal much—just some dusty cardboard boxes, broken lawn mowers and a few moldy straw bales.

A flash of green and red seared through the windows, followed a few seconds later by a loud crackling sound. The sun wasn't even down yet, but the good people of Cherry didn't waste any time when it came to celebrating the nation's birthday.

Before he left town, Hammond promised his son that this year would be different, that he'd be there this time to watch "the fire boomers." If he didn't get himself in gear, Davie would be crushed. Again. He decided to perform a quick sweep of the shed and then scoot his boots down the road. The heat in there had started to choke him out. And then there was that smell—the sickening sweet-and-sour of death and something underneath, like the lion cages at the zoo.

He stopped when he saw a human form on the floor a dozen feet in front of him.

"Well, shit," said Hammond as he approached the old man's corpse, which lay face down in the dirt. Pools of blood flanked his midsection like like obscene wings. Kneeling down, he grabbed the body by the shoulder and wrenched it onto its back. What was left of Miles Brody's abdominal cavity reminded Hammond of the cattle mutilations he'd seen over the past few weeks. It was a growing problem nobody in Cherry wanted to acknowledge with more than threats toward the local coyote population. Whatever had disemboweled the old guy had also plucked his eyes out of the sockets and sliced off his nose, leaving only his mouth intact, which hung open in mute protest. Red and blue lights blossomed outside and glinted off the old man's teeth. Soft reports followed.

That monkey-house smell grew stronger still. Ragged breaths filled the air behind Hammond.

He barely had time to turn around before it was on him, ripping into his insides just the way it had done to Miles Brody. His only shot went wide before the thing reached one of its malformed limbs to knock the pistol away. Then the other hand fell to the ground, still clutching its flashlight. Thus disarmed, Hammond screamed and battered the creature's moist skin with his gushing stumps as the creature continued its deadly work. Wet sounds, like a serving spoon moving through his wife's famous macaroni salad (which she brought to the pot luck earlier in the afternoon), echoed off the shed's thin walls.

More colorful blossoms filled the shed's windows when the thing pinned him to the dry ground and brought its smooth, broad face up close to Hammond's. As he faded into oblivion, Hammond watched little stars—blue, green, red and yellow—cavort and dance deep within the thing's vast black eyes. I made it to the fire boomers, Davie, he thought. I made it this year.

THE SCENIC PATH OF HUMAN ARTEFACTS

Cate Gardner

You arrive at a fork in the road and you have a choice.

A Buddha statue tells you that your path lies to the left, noting that said path is leafy, dark and plain creepy. Beside him, a man with a guitar points to the right advising you to take the populated route with its souvenir shops, tourists, alien artefact museum and security cameras.

You listen to Buddha, right? Because the guy with the guitar, well he has no face.

Anita found the sneaker a little way down the path. Its sole covered in mud, its laces gnawed, and the foot that had once inspired movement severed at the anklebone. At that point, screaming was redundant. A sword swept out of the dark to sever her vocal cords. Anita's disembodied head spun at dizzying speeds and landed nose down in the dirt. Unfair, she thought. Now she couldn't scowl at her attacker.

A hand gripped hold of her ponytail and picked her up, dangling her in front of his face. The last remnants of her spit travelled across the air to land on his bulbous nose, his snot dripped blue, his tears welled green. Adding insult to obvious injury, he jammed her head down onto a branch—it scraped against her brain—and stepped back to take a photograph. A Polaroid—the guarantee of instant humiliation.

In a bizarre twist on the 'who am I?' game, her attacker stuck a post-it note on her forehead and the photograph of her rotting head on his. He sat and stared at her, while she just stared. She wanted to ask, "If I get it right, will you sew my head back on?"

The shake of his confirmed he was telepathic and unsympathetic. Several of the arms attached to his coat waved their fists at him. The non-blue tinge to their skin confirmed they'd once belonged to humans. Anita recognized the deer tattoo on the hand beating against the attacker's chest. It confirmed that Red had not walked out on her.

I'm not playing. She pulled her tongue at the blue man and found she couldn't pull it back in. She felt sick to her phantom stomach. Fall leaves dislodged with the shake of her head and the twig prodded into her brain. A few memories dissipated with the act, but sight, hearing and pain remained.

He pressed Red's fingers to the Polaroid and pointed at her. If her fingers weren't digging into the dirt, she'd rip off the post-it note and point at him.

And I am what became of your kind. She blinked.

He nodded and pulled her head off the branch when she would prefer he slammed his fist down on her skull and ended this. Perched beneath his B.O. soaked underarm, and deaf from the press of stolen flesh against her earlobes, Anita joined him in the journey back to the path's beginning. The man, he of the wise advice, continued to rest against his guitar, and she now saw that it was jammed into his butt and their attacker had pasted his missing face to Buddha's backside.

The alien placed her head in Buddha's lap, and then he waddled back down the path to wait for the next fool.

A duo of giggling girls stopped to take photographs of Anita's head—now she was a celebrity—and the Guitar Man's faceless skull. Their sneakers tripped against the yellow lead and woke Buddha. The sage advised them to take the scenic path.

HANDOVER

Brendan Carson

I come into the ER, wet from rain. Bulmer looks up. "The late Doctor Robinson," he says.

"Sorry," I say. "You seen Donna? She didn't come home."

"She was around," Bulmer gestures vaguely. "It's been busy." Bulmer turns to the interns. "Doctor Robinson is senior on the morning shift. Run everything past her. She has a particular liking for the mad, the malodorous and the malingering."

I grin and shake my head. "Who've we got?"

It's first shift for the new interns, and night shift in Emergency can be hell. Sometimes I think I should have done Psych like Donna. She's on one night in twenty, I'm one night in four. It's hard to keep a relationship going. The screen is full. It's been a busy night. Bulmer starts handover.

"Cubicle one is a sixty two year old man, viral pneumonia, stable on four litres oxygen..."

The new interns scribble copious notes, the others jot a word or two. The litany rolls on. Bulmer hands over the unstable cases himself, lets the interns (nervous, occasionally stammering) do the others. I smile, thank them, try to sound less impatient than I am. The last intern is squat, muscular, a thin film of sweat over his face. For a moment he seems oddly familiar. His lab coat hides his name-tag.

"Cubicle forty," he starts, "is a thirty two year old man, detained under the mental health act as a danger to himself or others, with a long history of a schizophreniform illness. Since his early teens he..."

Bulmer looks up, irritated.

"We'll see him first," I say. "Tell me as you walk over there."

Away from the other doctors he seems more nervous, more sweaty. He checks his notes as he walks. "Classic erotomanic psychosis, resistant to diagnosis and therapy,

67

delusions about his female neighbours spying on him, inserting erotic thoughts into his head, she's the one to blame for all his symptoms. Previous diagnoses paranoid subtype—"

"In emerge," I say, "we don't care about all that developmental history stuff, how his mom molested him with a carrot or whatever."

He looks surprised. "But what—"

"It's all about problem solving."

He nods, like he understands. We reach the secure cubicle. I swipe my card, "So, briefly, what are we doing with him?"

"He's for psych review today," says the intern.

I shake my head. Psych are meant to review all emergency patients on day of admission. They act like seeing patients will kill them. I can say that because I live with one.

Inside the room is silent, simple. The thick door hisses shut behind us. No windows, a single light. A low stimulus environment keeps things quiet for all of us. The patient is a shape beneath the blankets.

"Medically stable?" I say over my shoulder. The intern is doing something with the keypad.

"Medically, he's very strong."

I glance over at him. It's a strange thing to say. The patient hasn't moved. The intern steps forward.

"Here." He grins. "I'll introduce you."

He reaches past me. He twitches the blanket away.

I stare. It's not a patient, it's Donna, and she's dead. My heart thumps in my chest, I feel like I'm going to be sick. I turn. I'm shaking so I can hardly stand.

Behind him, I see the keypad, hanging by a flex.

"She got me in a lot of trouble," says the new doctor. Now I remember his face, dark and suspicious, his door closing as we opened ours, across the apartment hallway. "But you won't, will you?"

And then I see the blood beneath his fingernails.

THE FARMER'S DAUGHTER

Jeremy Kelly

He kept her heart in his hands when it wasn't in the barn, and he made her dance for him when he held it to remind him of what he'd lost.

He liked being a farmer. It was an old trade, an inevitable transition for someone who is endless. You can't make your way through life with magic alone, after all. Magic was too conspicuous, too unexplainable. Farming was not. Farming was idyllic.

His wife, the last of dozens, eventually left. He forced her out finally, and he sealed any possibility of her return with a binding spell. It was an unfortunate consequence, but a necessary one should the little girl be raised as one who is endless. This was all before the little girl was old enough to remember. So that made it good.

The little girl loved to dance around the farmhouse. It was the only trace of her mother that remained.

He loved her more than the world since the day she was born. They were inseparable.

She was his first—a funny thought, given the fact that he was two centuries old and well able.

He raised her himself. He bore her proud upon his shoulders when they rode into town. She learned her way about the farm at a very young age. She loved her father more than anything else that could possibly exist in her little world.

They were alone together and very happy.

Inevitably, she turned fourteen.

And she met a boy.

She told him that she had fallen in love. He told her that, in time, she would come to find the notion of love ridiculous. Their kind did not fall in love with strangers.

She told him that she did not believe in being endless. There was only now. He forbade her from such blasphemy.

She stopped talking to him about the boy.

Life went on, but quieter. There was no more music. She told him that she had forgotten how to dance.

She didn't sit with him on the porch in the late afternoons as she had always done. She grew nervous around him at the supper table. He sensed that she had begun to wander away in her soul.

One morning, he woke early to bale the hay.

He found them in the barn. He found her naked with straw in her hair, curled up fast asleep in the arms of the boy that she thought she loved.

He snapped and before he knew it, a good bit of his old self made things known within the world again.

He snapped his fingers and her heart exploded from her chest into his hands before she had time to wake. The boy saw the blood pour from the wound in her breast and screamed like a little boy does until he made a sign in the air and closed the boy's throat from the inside. He lifted the boy from the ground and threw him so hard that it sent him through the roof into the sky so far up that the boy's people never found the body.

The girl eventually opened her eyes. They were milky white and sightless. She stared after her own beating heart in his hands, and she followed it stumbling back into the house.

Inside the house he wept for her. He sat in his chair in the dark before dawn and whispered for her to dance and she did, twirling naked around him through the shadows, the gaping hole in her chest empty and throbbing black blood, until the sun began to rise and he felt like things were right again.

In the early hours, he locked her and her heart in separate corners of the barn and went about his chores.

When the sun fell, so did his heart, so he drew hers out again. She followed.

Things went on this way for many, many nights, until he eventually died of a broken heart. She took her heart back from him but the damage was done, so she held it in her hands and she stumbled as she wandered away from him for the last time.

She met a violent end, finally, at the hands of those who do not know magic and are afraid of things they cannot explain—an unfortunate ending to an endless tale.

THE WRONG THING TO SAY
Jonathan Pinnock

Father Skerritt was enjoying his first solo exorcism. The young girl was writhing about on the bed with considerable energy, and it took both her parents to hold her down. She was blaspheming away like a Clydeside stevedore and producing some spectacular projectile vomit. And it might have been a trick of the light, but he was convinced that her head had rotated a full 360° at one point. This was the full Monty.

And yet, in the middle of it all, he was calm. He felt serene. He had a hotline to the Boss, and he was ready to make the connection.

"In the name of the God the Father, God the Son and God the Holy Ghost, release this poor girl from her travails—"

"Fuck you bastard!" said the ten-year-old girl.

"—go now and leave her in peace—"

"Fuck you!"

"—depart from this world into the shadows—"

And then it happened. The girl gave one final contortion and began to hemorrhage. As she shrieked in agony, her belly was torn open and a revolting reptile poked its head out. With a malevolent squawk, the beast forced the rest of its body through and hurtled out of the room.

When reflecting on it later, it struck Father Skerritt that "Whoa, mash-up!" was probably an inappropriate thing to say at this point. But he still couldn't help thinking that it was massively cool.

AFTERTASTE
Karen Schindler

She was exquisite.

Her naked body seemed to pulse and thrum as he circled her, snapping image after image, the afterglow of her pale form burning into his retinas. His mind reeled as he captured her likeness. He'd never worked with someone who looked so luminous through the lens.

He kept snapping and circling and circling and snapping convinced that he could see heat rolling off her in waves. He could feel her energy feeding his as he revolved closer and closer. When they came face to face for the last time she widened her eyes and made a sound that was as close to a groan as he could bear and remain upright.

He felt a jolt of something run top to bottom through his nerve endings. He wanted to reach for her but he couldn't stop snapping images. He couldn't tear his face away from the camera.

Mesmerized, he watched as her left hand reached out to caress the long shaft of the telephoto lens. Her right beckoned with a delicate finger.

He leaned toward her, her face getting larger in the viewer until it filled every corner of his vision and his mind. She tipped her head, licked her lips and parted her mouth into an inviting O.

He felt himself drawn into and through the prisms of the camera, out the lens and into her mouth.

As his body crumbled away she gently placed the camera onto the floor. She licked a finger and delicately sampled the pile of dust that had been a man moments before.

She smiled, languidly stretched and savored the memory card melting on her tongue just as a devout Catholic savors a holy communion wafer.

She could feel his juices mingling with hers, feel his hot blood soaring in her veins. He had been a good one.

Young, vital, full of sexual power. He should last her for at least a month.

The happy accident of a wave depositing her into a time plane that sported photographers on every corner and the internet to help her find them made it so easy. She hardly even had to hunt.

The only downside was the memory cards.

She just couldn't get used to the digital aftertaste.

THE WIND WHISPERS MY NAME
Jameson T. Caine

At night the wind calls to me, whispering my name. I lie in bed, eyes closed, desperate for the solace of sleep, but it eludes me. As I drift away into fitful slumber, the soft sound of the breeze brushing against my window stirs me from my repose, my name carried to me through the surrounding darkness.

It speaks with her voice.

I do not look, afraid of what I might see...or what I might not see. It couldn't be her, not after all this time. Not after that last, horrible night. To find her standing there now beyond the frail glass would surely drive me insane, yet the thought of throwing aside the curtains and seeing nothing frightens me even more.

I recall her final words, spoken in anger, defiance and finally, hatred. The way her pleas and denials became an antagonistic admission of truth, her fury boiling over, transforming once-beautiful features into the menacing snarl of a stranger. The elegant face I knew so well now a terrifying visage of rage and malevolence. Forever will I remember the look those icy eyes had cast my way seconds before the light within them was extinguished forever.

Or not.

Had she somehow survived? I took such care in disposing of the gun and locating a suitably remote place to bury her horrid remains. She was dead, I'd made sure of it. In all the intervening years, I have had no cause to doubt the outcome of that night. Still, after three sleepless nights haunted by the sound of her voice upon the wind, I had to be sure.

I came to the ancestral cabin in which we spent that fateful evening, high atop a bluff overlooking the restless sea. By day I searched the nearby woods, looking for her final resting place. But time wasn't kind to the land or to my memories. I could not find her.

Can the vow made before her death be coming true? Could she even now be drawing upon dark, arcane forces to enact the promised revenge from somewhere beyond the realm of the living? I push aside such thoughts as fanciful imaginings, but when darkness engulfs the land and the wind rises, I think differently. I recall the unholy things she did and the lives ended through her deeds; all performed under the watchful eyes of the one whom she called Teacher. How could I not put an end to such evil when I finally learned of it?

Night has come again. I huddle inside, a fading fire my only source of warmth and illumination. The wind rises and falls outside, her voice a whisper and then a shattering scream. I dare not look through the window, for I know the only thing I will find is my end.

I cover my ears but the shrieking gale cannot be denied. I scream, desperate to drown out her mournful cry with the ragged sound of my own voice, but my tortured howls cannot overcome the intensity of that ghastly lamentation. The wind has become her voice, throwing my own name back at me in accusation and anger.

I hurl the door open, determined to heave myself from the cliff to the cold waters below. I stagger towards the edge, my fear of death at war with my desire for this madness to end. It's then that I see her, standing a few feet from the ledge, waiting.

The one whom she'd called Teacher.

Teacher looks at me, eyes dark and penetrating. "You will replace the servant you took from me," she says.

And I know that I will. Her voice is commanding, insidious. I must not disobey. I eye the nearby ledge, but the wind keeps me from jumping, blowing in off the sea and forcing me back, preventing my demise at my own hand. It pushes me forward into the embrace of the soulless thing before me and I scream with unbridled terror when I peer into those dark eyes, seeing the fate awaiting me.

Taunting and cruel, the wind laughs at me in her

76

voice, the one I killed that night so many years ago. The one whose face I still see when I look in the mirror.

The one whom I called twin sister.

JEFF, NEWMAN'S, HEADACHES,

Alan Baxter

The only interesting thing about Jeff Newman was his headaches. Never a particularly social animal, Jeff lived alone in a small apartment in a grubby city. He worked for a nondescript company doing largely irrelevant administrative roles and took his pay home every month to spend on DVDs, video games and take away food. He was boring. But he did get such headaches.

He could tell when a headache was coming on. He would start to feel nauseous, the back of his neck would tighten up and get hot. He would feel as though his right shoulder was hitched up a couple of inches and he couldn't relax it, almost as if the base of his skull was trying to suck the rest of him up into his brain pan. Then the eye thing would start. Initially a kind of dull pinch behind his right eyebrow, it would grow until it felt like a sickening bruise all around his eye and he'd get a grabbing, stabbing compression, as if his brain had grown a hand, taken hold of his eyeball and started to squeeze. That was when he had to shut everything off. He would go into his bedroom, draw the curtains, turn off the light and lie in swimming, excruciating darkness, unable to rest, simply enduring. Eventually the vomiting would start, great deep heaves from the depths of his gut. Gasping, eye-watering retches until he brought up nothing but gobs of yellow bile and finally collapsed, exhausted, into blank, black sleep, not dreaming or stirring.

When he woke the headache would be gone, his brain releasing its hold on his eye, and he would feel purged. Weak, wobbly, trembling with the slightest effort. He would give anything to be rid of the headaches.

"It's stress, Jeff. The tension builds up and causes the headache. We've discussed this before."

78

Jeff shook his head, looking at his doctor with disdain. "It's not stress. I'm not a stressed person."

The doctor smiled. 'Everyone has stress. How often is it happening?'

"It used to be only once or twice a year at most. Now it seems like it's happening every few weeks. I can't handle it."

"I'm going to prescribe you something to help you relax." The doctor held up a placatory hand at Jeff's expression. "Process of elimination."

Jeff shook his head but sat quietly while the doctor wrote the prescription. He passed the pharmacy on his way home and took a pill as soon as he got in. By seven pm his brain had a hold on his eyeball and he squirmed and thrashed on his sweat-soaked sheets, cursing the doctor with every heartbeat that pulsed lightning through his head.

"I'm sorry, you can't see Doctor Steed." The receptionist's eyes were puffy and red. 'He... he's not available."

Jeff frowned. "When will he be available?"

"I'm afraid he won't be. He..." The receptionist trailed off into sobs.

A female doctor appeared. She patted the receptionist's shoulder. 'Go home, Jennifer. It's too much to ask you to work today.'

Jennifer hurried from her desk, grabbing bag and coat as she scurried, snivelling, for the door. The female doctor turned to Jeff. "I'm sorry. Dr Steed was killed last night. Home invasion. I'd be happy to see you if it's urgent."

"No. No, nothing urgent." Jeff stared at the doctor for a moment then turned to leave. "I'm sorry," he added over his shoulder as he reached the door. The female doctor nodded once, lips pursed.

Jeff sat on the bus staring at trees whipping past. How many people did he know that had died? It seemed

79

uncanny that so many people he was acquainted with had met strange, grim ends. His doctor killed in a home invasion, his last boss murdered while jogging at night, that stuck up bitch at the video store killed in a botched robbery... Jeff's heart began to hammer as a hot fist pushed its way up his throat. His mouth popped open as he gasped for air. But he'd had so many more headaches than that...

"Strangers are just as sweet."

Jeff whimpered, stiffening on the rough fabric seat of the bus. "What the fuck...?"

"Took you long enough to realise. But there's nothing you can do." The voice was high and sharp, laced with malice, echoing through his mind. Each word was punctuated by the sensation of a tiny hand flexing its grip on Jeff's right eyeball.

MILK OF THE GODDESS

Brendan P. Myers

I was six weeks into a yearlong contract for American Oil, working a desert outpost south of the border. At night, I went to Pablocito's and drank pulque, the milky liquor favored by the locals.

The girl was seventeen and slinging drinks, with only the barest hint of Indian in her milky complexion. She smiled shyly while fending off the drunken advances of my boorish colleagues.

When Larsen reached out to grope her, she flashed a look my way. Filled with liquid courage, I walked over and popped him one. After that, drinks were on the house.

Later, we walked the dusty streets of town. In the shadow of the lecheria, I took her in my arms and then took her to my hotel. It was her first time.

Her name was Mayauel, named after the milk tree Goddess, the Goddess of pulque and childbirth, the foundation of all life. In bed, she whispered reverently of the Goddess's four hundred breasts that suckled her human offspring. I grabbed her playfully and said two were enough.

We met furtively, exchanging glances in the bar, later sneaking off to my hotel. I knew she was falling in love. I didn't know what love was. And then it happened.

She said she was with child. I got angry and said it wasn't mine. I called her a whore and stormed off.

I moved to a rooming house close to the worksite. But every night, after closing my eyes, I saw her face. Her stare grew harsher with each passing day. I kept my eyes open most nights.

They sent me into town one day for a delivery. Avoiding once-familiar streets, I snuck in the back way and heard music playing. Sad music. At the end of a darkened alley, I saw a procession. Hysterical women dressed in black. Pablocito crying. An open casket on the back of a wagon. I caught a glimpse of her face and ran.

I hitched as far away as I could, but there was no escaping her. In one sleepy town, I saw a mural of a many-breasted woman in peach garment, with white fringe and flame colored hair. She was seated on a throne of a turtle and a snake, holding out a bowl filled with a milky substance.

The Goddess. Mayauel.

I staggered toward the center of town and saw a church. I knew then I needed forgiveness.

Inside, blinding sunlight streamed through stained glass, turning the holy chamber orange and red and yellow. Halfway to the altar, I collapsed and prostrated myself before God.

Begging forgiveness, I crawled down the aisle, finally raising my head toward the marble pulpit and whitewashed stone of delicately carved archways and saw then I wasn't alone.

It was Mayauel. My Mayauel.

Twenty-feet tall and growing taller by the second.

Sunlight set her hair aflame. Sitting astride the pulpit, she wore a peach dress with white fringe. But this Mayauel did not offer sustenance. Instead, I watched as she poured a bowl filled with the milk of human kindness onto the floor, where it pooled like a sea of bitter tears. For me, there would be no forgiveness.

UN ULTIMO HOMBRE LOBO

Adam Blomquist

"Action," yelled the fat man standing behind the camera.

Maria, the gorgeous Italian, pushed the intricate Gothic candelabra into Molina's face.

"Closer," said the director.

Molina frothed at the mouth and growled at the young actress. The film was a period piece so Maria wore a corset that threatened to suffocate her with her own cleavage. She backed Molina as far into the corner as he could go. The film was shooting on location in an ancient castle on the coast of Portugal, and the stone wall felt pleasantly cool against Molina's back.

"Closer, try to burn him," cried the director.

Molina stayed in character even though he could now smell burnt hair. The prosthetic fur on his face was beginning to go up in flames.

"Cut, cut," he slapped the cameraman on the shoulder. "Molina, what the hell are you doing? Where is the anguish we discussed? I expected more from the supposed master of monsters," Marques wagged a dark stubby finger in Molina's face who allowed himself to stay a bit in character and bared his fangs at the director.

"I'm sorry, it's your film, we'll do it again," Molina said with no sincerity in his voice.

"Forget it, we're losing daylight as it is," Marques said. Why the director was shooting a scene with a werewolf that needed daylight was beyond Molina, and he laughed at the director's ignorance. Marques did not take notice and turned his attention to the girl.

"And you, where is your fire? Where," Marques asked. Molina couldn't help but scoff at the pomposity in his voice. The director was wasting his time anyway. The girl spoke absolutely no Spanish and her translator had failed to show up to work today.

In fact, much of the crew had quit in recent days. Molina looked around the set and took a quick roll call. Inside the chamber there were only the two actors, the cameraman, Marques and a production assistant who had been promoted to a soundman for the day.

"Don't yell at her, she's doing the best she can," Molina's public persona was that of the perfect gentleman, and he had attained that persona by actually being a perfect gentleman. Maria had no idea what the two Spanish men were arguing about, but she knew that Molina was on her side. He gave her a wink and watched her blush.

"Grazie," she said.

Marques looked over at the impromptu soundman, who was leaning on the boom microphone as a cane. The director started histrionically pulling at his balding scalp and cursing under his breath. In his excitement he yelled that the day was wrapped and then stormed off the set.

The remaining crew members began to strike all the equipment and pack it back in the truck for the night. Molina went back to his trailer and began to gingerly remove his makeup. He needed the makeup artist in order to apply it but he had mastered the art of taking the pieces off himself without damaging them. It was a lengthy process and he began to let his mind wander to Maria.

He then took out the fake dentures and his mind turned to that toad of a director. Dusk was finally complete and he could see the full moon outside his trailer window. He ran his tongue over his teeth. The actor laughed to himself as his real fangs started to elongate and sharpen. Hair began to sprout on his arms. I think it's time for Marques to retire, we don't need him. And anyway, I've always wanted to direct, he thought to himself. Maybe I'll try some Italian for dessert.

FLASH CARDS FOR THE BLIND

Kurt Newton

These are not your average 4x6s. Instead of an equation on one side, a solution on the other, these thin rectangles are virtually featureless. They look more like opaque panes of glass...without the sharp edges, of course. That would be cruel.

(You fidget slightly. I know the feeling. Trust is a difficult commodity nowadays...rare in its purest form.)

"Then how do they work?"

(Your eyes stare past me. Though blind, they appear eager, open to new experiences.)

Well, they work the way a window works, only instead of using the sensory organ designed for sight, it uses something much more intimate: touch. It is the reason I am wearing these specially designed gloves. Just the slightest skin-to-surface contact induces a chemical transference that affects the region of the brain responsible for perception. Touching is seeing.

"What will I see?"

(A smile graces the corner of your mouth. It informs me I have chosen well.)

Ah, that's the beauty. It is entirely up to you. The mystics say if you stare at your reflection long enough your true essence will eventually reveal itself. Perhaps you will see your own death. Perhaps you will witness the torture of the innocent, or the savagery of nature, or the oppressive immensity of the universe. Perhaps you will be whisked away to a place unknown, a place forbidden, a place where your darkest fears dwell. A place where truth lies bound and screaming.

(You swallow your last naïve notion. Your fingers tremble as I place the first card in your hands.)

"And my blindness will be cured by doing this?"

Yes. But you will wish it hadn't.

RARE STEAKS, BLACK AND BLUE

Rachel Green

Luisa browsed the menu again. She'd been ecstatic last June when she'd found this exclusive little steak house tucked into an alley off Manhattan's East 67th Street. Bored with the standard fare of beef, buffalo and venison, the restaurant promised gastronomic riches. Tattooed waiters and waitresses of several nationalities catered for the high-class clientele.

She'd picked and chosen for the first few visits. It was expensive but the rarity of springbok, kangaroo, giraffe and zebra was worth the expense. She was more methodical after that, working her way through the menu one visit at a time, every steak cooked black-and-blue, just how she liked it, with sauces on the side, never on the meat.

After thirty visits her palate was jaded and she sat at her customary booth flicking listlessly through the menu. Peter, the only waiter still working there since she'd found the place, stood poised with his pencil and pad. "I want something different," she said, "something really unusual."

"I know just the thing," Peter said. "A chef's special, Yes?"

She smiled and handed back the menu. "That sounds divine."

It took a little longer to prepare but every morsel was worth the wait. Tempted as she was, she left the strip of fat and the edge of skin.

She'd recognised the tattoo.

BESIDE HIMSELF

Joe Nazare

Forget that heals-all-wounds nonsense—time for him to expedite matters. He can't bear any longer to just let such grotesquerie be.

So, thrumming with impatience, he extends his right index, and with his left hand picks up the smallest of the tools lying atop the butcher block. He clamps the tweezers to his blueberry-shaded nail, the concentrated bruising of his fingertip making him think of a well-fed tick squashed under a microscope slide. In its protracted death throes, the nail has pinched inward into the shape of a miniature seashell, but naturally he has no intention of holding the thing up to his ear afterward.

Plugging the tip of his tongue into his gums, he tugs at his blighted digit. The fingernail pulls forward slightly before rebounding into place. He tries again, and again, but on the third try the tweezers slip off, etching a hairline white scratch on the nail. Frustration rattles in the base of his throat as he tosses aside the useless tool.

So close. The taunting words echo in his head. He grabs the pair of slip-joint pliers and applies them to the task at hand. Like the lips of the most unyielding pistachio, the fingernail offers only a few millimeters of airspace between itself and flesh, but the pliers' bulkier pincers nonetheless manage to find a grip.

He steels himself with a quick series of snorts, then jerks the pliers back hard as he can. A dull ache radiates down his finger and seemingly right into his forearm. The nail feels like it has grown tendrils, and for a moment he wonders if in tearing free it will yank a trailof ligaments out through his fingertip—the physical equivalent of some magician's handkerchief trick. He pulls on the nail regardless, relentless, and after several tormenting seconds finally succeeds in the extraction.

The nail un-suctions itself from his fingertip and drops clattering to the butcher block.

He pays scant attention to the pearly nub of new growth on his right index, focusing instead on the brittle relic just removed. Slit-eyed, he picks up and turns over the unfastened nail. The blue-black grue caked to its underbelly looks like what you might find inside an old tin of shoe polish.

Another moment of intrigued scrutiny, and then he pivots and limps across the basement, into the corner occupied by the cyanotic clay effigy. This inert reflection of himself, painstakingly dusted with his own dead skin. It stands grinning at him through an imperfectly aligned set of grayed teeth. He splits his sunken mouth into a smile as he presses the fingernail into place at the tip of a crooked index. The transplant accomplished, he turns and scurries back to the butcher block.

So close, he tells himself again. Spurred by the sudden, unmistakable crack of knuckles off to his left, he seizes and raises his trusty ball-peen hammer.

And gets started on his right thumb.

DARKLING
Christopher Green

The loss of Marion's vision was a gradual thing.

By degrees, the edges of her sight slipped away, the world to her left and right made into old friends she thought of occasionally but never missed. She saw her home, her husband, and, less and less, her children and their children, through a circle that grew ever tighter, like a noose.

When she began to trade paint with nearby cars in parking lots, she left the driving behind and taught herself to take the bus. She made arrangements for the grocer to deliver the week's groceries on Thursdays.

This Thursday, when the doorbell rang, Marion made her way to the front of the house by touch. She brought her handbag, to pay Mr. Williams, but by the time she opened the door he'd already gone, leaving the groceries on the front step. She brought the bags inside one at a time.

In the bottom of one, next to the milk, was the darkling. It was a spot, a smear, no more than a tear in the light, and it slid around in the vast dark corners of her vision. It went with her into the family room, watched her soaps with her, and when Stan got home smelling like beer, the darkling slipped closer to Marion, where Stan's vision had always been weakest.

Stan ignored them both.

When he went to bed, the darkling had already found a little to eat, scraps, old glances and smiles and even a kiss Marion or Stan or both had let fall behind the couch. The thing was bigger, now, and bolder, and when it strayed from the corners of her sight she didn't notice. The room had never been well lit, and the television threw flickering shadows that let the darkling, if it was quick and cunning, as all dark things are, roam the floor and find other things to eat.

When Marion finally saw it, the darkling froze. By now, near to midnight, it knew Marion enough to call her mother, if it called her anything at all. When it crawled up beside her on the sofa, its thick hide slick with lost recollections, she lay her hand against its bulk.

"Hello, there," she said aloud, and the darkling quivered with joy. "What have we here?"

The darkling had no voice.

"A friend," she said to herself, and pat it once or twice. "A friend at last, again."

The darkling fed her back a little of what it had found in the room, old Christmases and birthdays and nights she and Stan had stayed in together. She took what it offered and smiled to herself in the dance of the TV's light. The corners of the room held nothing for her, and the darkling at her side swelled as she fed it more of her wisps and fragments.

As it grew, the couch springs creaked like they did when Stan sat there. Marion smiled and took it by its new hand. She led it in to where Stan was sleeping. She would give it his voice, and let it remind her of the things she had let remain forgotten for far too long.

GOURMAND
Brad Nelson

Most of us will eat anything; we see food, we go for it—most of us. I'm picky. I prefer certain dishes. What? You may ask. How can you be picky? I've seen your kind, you say. Well, so have I, and as I said, most of us will eat anything. And, frankly, I am offended, Madame. I don't have time for your preconceived notions and prejudices. My kind? How could you be so insensitive to the feelings of others?

I have a theory about my preferences, my snobbishness as my brethren might think of it. Don't get me wrong; I don't know why I like what I like. It's more a theory of how than of why.

You see, when The Outbreak first crossed our borders, it came from the south, crossing from Mexico into the United States in the blood of drunken state-college students, American tourists, and Mexican immigrants. Drug dealers and human smugglers also helped. The Outbreak spread to college campuses, trailer parks, ghettos, barrios, and every corner of lower- and middle-class society—and it spread like fire, cleansing the land.

The average human being is led by simple desires, Maslow's Hierarchy of Needs. Have you heard of it? Physiology, safety, love, esteem, self-actualization? Any of this ring a bell? No? Anyway, you are driven by certain instinctual motivators. Once the most basic of those needs are met, such as physiological needs—breathing, food, water, sleep, homeostasis, excretion, etc.—a person may move on to the next tier, but not until the basic needs are met. Example: If your physiological needs are not met, if you do not have food, shelter, etc., you do not care about morality and creativity, which are needs at the very highest and intellectual level. Sadly, most people never attain those higher levels or even care to, which brings me to my next point.

The majority of those initially infected were of little or no means, and of little or no intelligence. What? You wonder about the drunken college students who brought The Outbreak to college campuses? I did say they were students from state colleges. You think students of Ivy League schools are spending spring break in Mexico? Come now, Ivy League mummies and daddies can afford better than that for their little sweetums.

You've gone and distracted me. Where was I? Oh, yes—intelligence. The average IQ in the United States is 100, give or take. Average IQ drops exponentially based on social class, geography, race, etc; and I'd wager that the average IQ of students in state-run institutions adheres to the national average. Community college? Much, much lower. So, you see, pre-infection, the average person wasn't very bright to begin with. And you've seen what The Outbreak does to the mental capacities of those it touches.

Given that the majority of those initially infected fell into a category with a below-average IQ, is it any wonder that when fulfilling their basic need, food, they ate what they saw, without discrimination? With the infected, Maslow's Hierarchy is obsolete. Food is their only need. It is no different with me. Food is still my only need, but, as I said before, I have preferences. My theory? I am getting to that, my child. Be patient.

Pre-infection, I had an IQ of 138. That's two points away from genius, you see. My theory is this: the effects of The Outbreak—aside from reanimation, imperviousness to pain, and the hunger—involve a reduction of one's IQ by a specific percentage based on pre-infection intelligence. What? You still don't understand? Then, here, let me show you, my dear.

Where others would come in moaning and carrying on, mobbing you, marring your beautiful flesh with gnashing teeth and clawing nails, I will take my time enjoying the juicy portions slowly. Don't worry. I stay above the neck; I'm old-fashioned that way. I will take your soft cheek first, and then your lips, your tongue.

Your eyes I will slurp with abandon. Blue eyes are truly delightful. Please stop screaming, child. It does not make the pain any less. Now I will peel back your scalp, because I don't like getting hair caught in my teeth, and crack your skull. The real treat, the one those other idiots can never stop asking for, is inside.

IMPRISONED
AJ Brown

Dim light shone through air holes in the dungeon's ceiling. Vlad sat in one corner, the darkness concealing him from his prey. Shallow breaths billowed upward, and he shivered in the cold, clenching his teeth to keep them from clattering.

The roach appeared in the dusty light. Tentative steps from the shadows led to a quick dart across the room and back into darkness.

Vlad shifted his weight, lowering his body into a crouch. With eyes long adapted to the black of the tunnel, he followed the roach's movements toward the crumbs of molded bread lying near him.

Again, the roach crawled from the shadows, stopping in the center of a patch of light. It was large—a couple of inches long—its brown shell dirty; long antennae twitched, feeling its surroundings.

"Come," Vlad whispered, cupped and lowered his hands to mere inches above the ground.

The roach scurried toward him, tickled Vlad's big toe. Vlad's breath caught, skin tingled as the bug crawled beneath his hand. With a quick swipe, he scooped up the insect. It squirmed, legs tickling Vlad's palm.

"Little bug, I name you Matthias."

The roach poked its head from between Vlad's thumb and index finger. The once-proud ruler laughed. "You can't escape me, Matthias. You have sinned against your king. For the crime of betrayal I sentence you to death by impalement."

Vlad stood and hobbled to the corner closest to one of the air holes. He lifted one of the many slivers of wood he had pulled from the giant door that kept him from escape. The roach squirmed.

A crooked grin split Vlad's face, and he drove the splinter into the roach's abdomen. Its legs moved fast,

94

trying to run; antennae twitched and its cerci vibrated wildly. Vlad pushed the small stake in further. He imagined the bug screaming, begging for mercy. He chuckled in delight, his chest heaving, tingling in excitement.

Vlad lowered the roach he named after the ruler who imprisoned him, made a hole in the dirt and set the stake's edge into the ground. In the dim light of the dying sun, he sat, watching the bug—watching Matthias—twitch and writhe in agony. His eyes glazed over as he scanned the many insects and rats he had impaled, each one given the name of an enemy, each one having died slowly.

He leaned his head against the wall, eyes fixed on the dying roach, his body quaking in ecstasy.

Hours later sleep found him. Cradled in her arms, he dreamt of thousands of crying, screaming boyers and princes, women and little children, all of them on stakes, all of them sliding, sliding...

THE HUNGRY OCEAN
Ken Muise

Walking along the breakwater, fighting the wind that tried to force her ocean-side, she counted her steps to the ladder as she had always done. When she was a girl, when she had started the counting, she could recall reaching the ladder somewhere around 250 steps. Now, as her body had grown wearier and her steps choppier she often didn't reach the ladder until after three-hundred steps.

The Atlantic exploded against the large granite stones, throwing icy water shrapnel against her. She tasted the salt from the cold water on her lips. It traced its way down her shirt.

When Steve died last year during a tuna trip she had stopped coming here, unable to bear the thought of walking this expanse without him. She always appreciated the way he would come with her on this walk. The ocean was a mundane part of his everyday life but to her it was a wondrous adventure.

Having had no children her decision was acceptable. Being a young widow it was understandable. Having lived two excruciating years without the only thing she had ever loved made it inevitable.

She would curse the ocean as it happened. Curse it for the suffering it had caused her husband and for the misery it had left her in.

She made it to the ladder on step two hundred and fifteen. She was in a hurry to die.

She climbed down, cove side, onto a piece of beach the tide was quickly consuming. Flakes of rust encrusted themselves into her palms and fingers.

It was calm. The ocean rippled like a pond and the pleasant sound of the wet sand crackling pleased her.

She entered the small cave where the dinghy was stored hoping after all this time it was still there. She remembered the count. Six steps in and the dinghy would be there in the diminishing light.

There was no dinghy.

She walked further into the opening hoping that her age had altered her count as it usually would do on the breakwater. At ten steps in she knew she couldn't that be far off but still no dinghy.

There was a stirring from a few feet farther in.

She heard a thump to her left and slightly in front of her.

She backed up slowly.

Another thump into wet sand closer this time to her right.

In the faint light she saw a single webbed claw of grey-green scales with talons long and yellow. She heard a low throaty growl like a lion with a mouthful of water and a single yellow eye with no pupil opened suddenly reflecting the sunlight behind her.

The beast lunged and bit into her midriff, thrashing it's head wildly, ripping her in two and throwing pieces of her out of the opening in its ferocity.

The beast dragged the large pieces back into the cave methodically.

The tide would wash away the blood.

FAMOUS. MONSTERS. REMAKE!

Joe L. Murr

The Celebrity Bimbo sneaked through the dark forest. Right on cue, the Wolfman popped out from behind a tree, a machete held high in his hairy paw. The Celebrity Bimbo assumed a fighting stance and let out a battle cry.

"Cut! You call that a scream?" the director bawled.

The crew cracked up. The Celebrity Bimbo gave them the stink-eye. "What's so funny?" she said. The crew laughed twice as hard.

The director was the only one who was not amused. Eight crappy takes of the same shot. The actress wasn't even trying. At this rate they'd be stuck in the forest until dawn. "Honestly, was that the best you can do?" he said.

"Alan, I feel that she wouldn't scream." She put her hands on her waist. "She'd fight him. Punch him right in the face."

He leaned back in his canvas chair and rubbed the bridge of his nose. "It's not in the script."

"But maybe it should be."

Here we go again. Time to massage the ego. He went over to her. "Everyone, take a break."

Alan watched enviously as the Wolfman plopped a cigarette into his maw and flicked a Zippo, careful not to set his fur on fire. It had been two years since Alan quit, but now a coffin nail would be just what the doctor ordered.

The Celebrity Bimbo hissed, "Second-hand cancer." The Wolfman flipped her the bird.

Alan inhaled the drifting smoke and put his arm around her. "First of all, let Wolfie say his line. And then ...look, all I'm asking you to do is scream. Just a little scream. Like this: Eeee!"

"But, Alan, didn't we discuss my back story?"

Oh God had they ever. Or, rather, she had rambled on forever about how she saw the character while he nodded patiently.

"Her father was a Marine," she said. "He taught her how to survive."

"Be that as it may, in this shot she screams. Just give me one good scream. Or I'll have to cut your big dramatic scene."

She stared at him, shocked. "You wouldn't."

"Try me."

She nodded timorously.

"And remember to let Wolfie say his line, okay?"

He went back to his chair. Action—take nine. She approached the tree. The Wolfman popped into view and growled, "I'm gonna make you my bitch," a line that made Alan die a little inside, but the studio loved it, so ...

She gave a lackluster squeak.

"Better," he coaxed her. "Maybe with a bit of fear this time?"

They took it from the top. She approached the tree, peered around and unleashed the scream of the decade. Alan grinned. Until he saw what she was seeing. A rangy beast held the Wolfman's decapitated head in its claws. The Celebrity Bimbo fainted. And at that moment the lights went out.

People ran screaming into the woods. Alan scrambled out of his chair, slipped and fell on the wet grass. Hairy hands clamped around his neck and hauled him up. He stared straight into the creature's fetid maw.

A voice as old as mountains whispered, "You know what you've gone and done? You've turned me into a joke."

Alan struggled and squealed in animal panic.

"Once, we had power," the werewolf said, eyes gleaming yellow in the inky blue darkness. "We were iconic."

Things shuffled from the trees, wreathed in a charnel fog.

"Then you people started re-imagining us," one of them hissed through a mouthful of razor fangs.

A chorus of voices joined in:

"Taking from us our poetry and tragedy."

99

"No more sequels. No more remakes."

"We've had enough."

Alan saw his line producer, or rather what was left of him, in the hands of a brute swaddled in ancient bandages. Another monster wore the makeup artist's face as a mask.

"It's not my fault," the director gibbered. "My hands are tied. Blame the studio, the writer ..."

"We're going for them next," the werewolf growled.

Red lights started blinking. Lenses came in for a closer angle. Camcorders.

The werewolf said, "Action!"

The monsters fell on Alan and tore him to pieces.

And then they set out to teach film executives the real meaning of fear. The Mummy insisted on taking the Celebrity Bimbo along, believing that he had finally found the reincarnation of his lover. She screamed all the way to Los Angeles.

THE LAST CRUNCH OF AUTUMN

Patrick Rutigliano

Jamie Eisenberg was halfway down Crescent Avenue before the sight of his own breath stopped him cold. Jamie's run had no real aim, only pleasure, but the weather simply wasn't conducive to such activity.

Halloween was two weeks past and winter was already draining the color from the landscape. The days of snow forts and sledding had yet to arrive, and as the fire on the trees dulled and littered the streets with brown, he couldn't help but feel as though he was in the heart of something dying.

Neither Shane nor Jacob wanted to venture from their homes that day, and now, Jamie was beginning to realize they had the right idea.

What the hell could he do out here? Most of the neighborhood's overripe Jack-o'-lanterns were already smashed at the bottom of the quarry, and the cold demanded heavy coats and gloves that made sports more trouble than they were worth. All he could do was walk, and already a block from his house, he would have to do exactly that.

Turning the corner, Jamie stomped his way through a ridge of dead leaves on the side of the road. He hated them. Each footstep squelched, and not once did he hear the crunch of a proper autumn leaf. He took a moment to root through the debris with the toe of his sneaker before venturing on. Even the crickets were dormant.

Jamie knew the storm was to blame for most of it. The winds tore nearly all the remaining foliage from the branches, and the rain permeated the soil to the point of overflow. He could almost swear he felt the asphalt yielding underfoot.

Despite his mood, Jamie smiled as he reached Mr. Rutner's house. The man was a neat-freak, and everything around his place looked immaculate even after the squall. He might be good for a little fun later that night if he could sneak out without waking his folks. There were still a few eggs left in his Mischief Night stash he was dying to make use of.

Jamie was nearly beside the next yard when he noticed the mound of color earlier obscured by Mr. Rutner's hedges. The leaf pile looked tall enough to reach his waist, and even in the shadow of the greenery, Jamie could determine the quality of the leaves—dry, bright, and ready to be crushed by a falling body.

Jamie didn't know why Mr. Rutner hadn't bagged and hauled the leaves to the side of the road for pickup, but he didn't care either. It might be a bit childish, but nobody was watching, and neither Shane nor Jacob was there to tease him.

Jamie took one final look around to ensure his privacy and made a beeline for the pile.

As he raced forward and leaped into the air, he got the strange impression that the mound already had an imprint at its center. It was large, child-size, and he wondered if one of his friends might be as immature as himself as he landed at its core.

For a moment, he lay there panting. The crunch he was expecting was absent, and the leaves his hands rested on around the rim of the imprint felt harder than they should. He tried to squash one in his palm and failed, yelping instead as he felt blood trickle through the slit across his glove.

The wound distracted him. Jamie did not notice the slight tremor in the mound until the borders were already swelling over his head. His scream was muffled as he again felt something sharp bite through his clothing. Sinking deeper into the maw of the thing, he finally heard a crunch.

THE INSANITY VESSEL
Harper Hull

Neil shook on the sofa, knees pulled up, toes curled, watching his Gran swat away imaginary insects and invisible bats across on the other side of the room. She is just sick, his Mom always told him, just sick in the mind, no need to be frightened. He was constantly frightened, though. Gran saw things all over the place that no-one else could see. Things that no-one else would ever want to see. Each evening, as his Mom made dinner in the kitchen, Neil had to sit with his Gran in the living room and keep an eye on her, just to make sure she didn't wander or fall.

Gran told him awful, awful things. He tried not to listen, he told himself she was just sick, but she frightened him none the less. She told him about the shiny white people that visited her in the night, appearing inside her frilly old-lady clothes that hung in her wardrobe, growing into them until their long, bent fingers crept from the sleeves and whispering terrible words to her with their flapping black lips and flicking blue tongues until morning came. She told him about the long, wriggling snakes with human faces and the tiny, dark, snapping creatures that slithered and ran through the patterns in the carpet and the wallpaper, surrounding her and trying to bite her. Most of all, though, she told him about the heads in the fireplace that came up in the crackling orange flames and gave her messages. Messages that never seemed to make any sense. Sometimes the messages were for other people, but those other people were always dead people. His Dad. His Granddad. The poor old blind lady who had lived next door. More than anything else she talked about, Gran's talking fire heads scared him.

Neil hoped that Gran would stay busy shooing away the invisible flying things all around her and not pay attention to the spitting fire tonight. Remember, he told himself over and over, she is just a sick old lady; her brain doesn't work properly anymore. He didn't mind her so much when she was just slapping thin air. It was almost funny to watch. Almost.

Suddenly and inevitably Gran stopped flapping around in her saggy cloth armchair and became still, focusing her watery eyes on the popping, jumping fire. Neil groaned a little and wrapped his arms around himself.

"Oh Neil, they're talking about you tonight! All of them are looking at you and talking."

Neil forced himself to glance at the fire and, as usual, saw no speaking faces. His Gran was completely entranced in the flames, slowly nodding her head and cracking her thin, colorless lips. The stupid sickness, thought Neil again, her mind is broken. Remember!

"They say you're a bad boy, son. They say they see you doing things that a ten-year-old shouldn't be doing." Without averting her gaze, Gran feebly lifted one arm and pointed towards him, wagging one finger.

Neil looked back to the fire, wide-eyed. He couldn't see anything except the dancing flames and the hot, blackened wood glowing and splitting as it fuelled the tiny inferno. He knew he hadn't been a bad boy, the fire heads were lying. Silly, he immediately scolded himself, there are no fire heads, no people in the grate it's just her sickness, remember that always!

"They say they're going to get you Neil. They're going to get you tonight when you're asleep."

His Gran sounded unusually sad as she spoke. It pushed Neil past his breaking point and he jumped up and started walking towards the kitchen, to the safety of his Mom with her boiling vegetables, baking pie and roasting beef.

"They want you to know one last thing!" said his Gran, loudly now. "They say to tell you that I am not sick. They say I am not sick and my mind is not broken. Now why would they say that?"

Neil stopped dead in his tracks, legs like ice and face like fire, feeling his Adam's apple roll all the way down into his belly.

THE CHRONICLES OF BLACKBRIAR

Michael Colangelo

Jesus Christ, the Virgin Mary, St. Francis of Assisi, Joseph, the Virgin Mary. These are the gilded gold portraits that hang from the walls inside Nana's little apartment on Thanksgiving Day.

Blackbriar the Bear, Hamstring the Rabbit, Farmer Carrion—the names of the characters in the book tucked beneath little Peter's arm, The Chronicles of Blackbriar. These are his personal heroes.

He just wants to read his book, but this is a family get-together. They're celebrating an important, and holy, occasion. Great Grandmother sits in an armchair unblinking. The others chat and hug and drink around her. The men go out on the balcony to smoke and chat some more.

Uncle Vince picks Peter up, grinning. He places him on his knee. Peter gets a quarter from Vince's pocket and then he's offered the cigar hanging from Vince's mouth.

The smoke makes Peter cough and he doesn't like it. Uncle Vince just laughs and laughs. His face turns red he laughs so hard.

He makes sure he tells Peter's Mum and Dad that their kid likes cigars, just like he does. He makes sure to tell them that Peter is going to be just like him one day— a success.

Later on, after they eat dinner, Peter is tired. He rubs his eyes and sits on the couch while the adults move around him chatting and smoking and drinking some more. He's trying to read his book but it's so late that the colors in the pictures seem to smudge and the letters look all blurry.

The adults are ignoring him. They usually do. They're here to talk about adult things with one another. But Uncle Vince, as always, comes to help Peter out. He sits down beside him on the couch and takes the book from his hands.

He digs out his reading glasses and holds the cover up to the light.

"What is this, Peter? A book about a bear?"

He opens up the book and begins to skim through the pages. Near the end he begins to nod in understanding. His brow furrows like he's concentrating hard.

"Ah, so this bear. He goes to the farmer's house for dinner? Even after his friend the rabbit warns him not to do it?"

Peter nods. He's read the book before. He knows the ending. The last page of the book is a full page splash of Farmer Carrion and his wife all dressed up for a night on the town. The farmer's wife is wearing what's left of Blackbriar like a coat.

Uncle Vince turns serious. His face and his eyes grow very dark right before he leans over to whisper into Peter's ear. His breath smells of strong liquor.

"This bear, Peter. You know why the lady's wearing him at the end, right?"

Peter shakes his head.

"Because this Blackbriar's some kind of mother-fucker. That's why. Farmer Carrion, he just wants to take his wife out for dinner. Poor bastard can't afford to buy her nice things. Who can blame a guy for wanting the bear as a coat, eh?"

Peter shrugs and Uncle Vince gives a little laugh. Or maybe it's a growl. Peter's too tired. He can't tell.

"But the bear, he's just looking for a free meal. Some sort of handout. 'Don't be a motherfucker, Blackbriar'. That's what this rabbit is really saying. I don't think they're really friends. Do you?"

Then Peter's mother is standing over them both. She snatches the book from his lap and takes Peter up in her arms.

"But we were reading," Peter protests. He curls his head against her shoulder and then falls silent.

"We have to go, honey." She strokes his hair and takes him away from Uncle Vince.

It's later in the next year when Peter sees Uncle Vince again.

He's sitting on the front lawn with his old book in front of him when his dad pulls into the driveway. Behind him, a big black car with fins on it turns in and Uncle Vince gets out.

He's carrying a baseball bat. They're not about to play any baseball.

As Uncle Vince approaches, Dad turns to Peter and waves him off.

"Go inside, Peter. Uncle Vince and I need to talk."

Peter runs inside. His mother runs outside. Peter runs upstairs and goes under the covers of his bed with his book.

He reads for the one hundredth time about the time that Hamstring got caught in the fox trap. Blackbriar happily gnaws his rabbit friend's leg off to free him again.

KILLING FIELD
Brad Chacos

"He seemed like a decent enough guy," the neighbors said. Don't they always say that about killers?

They caught him eventually, in a sting operation. Only so many people, even hookers and junkies and street people, can be killed before Things Are Noticed. And they locked the man (if one can call him that) away for a hundred lifetimes, sentencing him to die the drawn-out gray death of boredom and certainty that his victims never had.

But they never found the bodies.

You may have noticed the field of wild roses outside of town, their petals drawn in on themselves, bright red and shivering in the autumn wind; once a month, when the moon is at its apex, they bloom in the cold, dark night, shedding dew like so many tears. And the smell... oh, *the smell...*

THE LISTENER

C.L. Scarr

Chill winds rolled off the tundra to steal each puff of Semyon's labored breath as he clamped the heavy collar onto the bit. He and Boris stepped back from the drillstring as it started rotating. Like a dog in heat, it plunged back into the hole.

"Do you think there's anything left?" Boris asked.

Viktor, their boss, hawked a wad of phlegm from the back of his throat and spat onto the barren ground. "You're not paid to ask questions about the meteorite. You're paid to drill."

They watched and waited while the drill retraced its path through the rock it had already bored. They smoked cigarettes, stamping their feet, hunching their shoulders against the cold.

"More slurry!" Boris shouted when the drill slowed as it bit deep into undrilled rock. Semyon turned to fetch another bag and pain filled his head. Sharp shrieking noises rose from the earth with the plume of fine grey silt. *Violation. Anguish.* He clutched the sides of his head. Through tear-filled eyes he looked to his drill crew for confirmation. They hadn't moved.

It wasn't until he sagged to his knees that the other crewmembers gathered around him. They carried him to the small tent where their six cots crowded together and laid him on his bed. As darkness battled the pain in his skull for control, voices mixed within and without. "...finally cracked..." "...hearing things..." Darkness finally won, and he slipped gratefully into its embrace.

Semyon woke in utter darkness and tried to gauge whether the pain from earlier in the day was gone. He sensed an uncomfortable remnant of it in the back recesses of his brain, slowly drifting away from him like the resistant tendrils of a dream.

Soft snoring surrounded him like a comforter, the crew resting after a hard day's work. It would take an explosion or the morning chow bell to wake them. He sat up and found his boots, then stepped carefully outside. A vague sense of unease, a balled rock of doubt in his stomach, told him that all was not as it should be.

He picked up the sledgehammer next to the drill rig and hefted it in his hands. The weight was comforting, solid. A voice whispered in his head, *Yes*.

He turned back to the tent. Semyon tried to stop, but his body refused to obey. Sweat beaded his brow in the chill night air as he struggled to control his body's actions without success. He watched like the passenger in the back of a car as he opened the tent flaps and secured them to let in the moonlight. He stepped inside.

Semyon's hands gripped the sledgehammer, his knuckles white against the sun-stained brown of his skin, then his feet carried him to stand over Viktor's cot. The arms raised up and brought the hammer down with a thud and a squelch on Viktor's head. Next it was on to Boris, and Pavel and Yuri and Mikhail.

The shaft of the hammer slipped from his grasp, sliding easily from his fingers due to the lubrication provided by blood and brain matter. Semyon stepped from the now quiet tent. He listened very hard. Over the sound of his pounding heart and panting breath came the memory song of the one trapped in the meteorite, disturbed by their drilling after so many years.

Primitive and victorious, it rang stronger and stronger from deep within. Semyon smiled.

MAID MARION
Scott Davis

Step/creak, step/creak, the rough wooden stairs Marion used to ascend to the sanctuary didn't make for a surprise entrance. But that was OK. Marion was resplendent in a ruched white gown, veil and bright red roses, to symbolize her true devotion. Marion felt like a princess. She was envisioning the damsels of old, strong but delicate, in children's stories. Real princesses met bad ends in French tunnels, but stark reality did not intrude on her reverie.

The wedding guests due to the long wait had run out of small talk and so resorted to discussing the latest news.

"Did you hear about planet Sargasso?"

"No, what?"

"They're going to colonize."

"But, it's only water! And, the sea life is primitive. Nasty predators!"

A third woman chimed in: "Excuse me, but I'm with Myth Engineering, and I can tell you they are well underway. The bioengineering folks are doing recombinant DNA for the Sargasso project. I'm working with Greek mythology about Neptune to provide cultural support for the shark people."

"Well, at least they didn't stray too far from Earth norms with us! We had to compensate for the lack of quality protein for fetal development here, but we aren't fish!"

As Marion reached the top of the stairs, all eyes turned and rose to behold her. She felt dizzy with all the attention, trying to maintain her balance in the surging sea of attention. She couldn't look down, or she would catch her legs in the hoops of her skirt, her mother had warned her.

Looking left or right was disorienting, so she looked ahead, where the minister and her beloved stood waiting. A ruffling sound that she imagined was angel's wings, sounded quietly, for this was a praying church. She made it to his side.

Wow, this is really happening, thought Marion, I'm really becoming an adult. Under her mother's loving gaze Marion stood and appeared to attend to the minister's words, but her own thoughts intruded. She caught snatches. "...as our progenitors of old Earth had done before us, he will supply the seed for new life as well as the nourishment to help the child grow..."

She hoped her wedding gown was hiding her changes, for Marion's body was growing in its excitement. How she wanted him! She remembered what her mother taught her about sex, to let him enjoy her fully, since he would never have a time like this again.

Her jaw loosened, reassuring her it would detach properly as she had prepared it to do in her pre-marital exercises. She quickly closed her mandibles demurely, since the minister was finishing up.

"You may now kiss the groom."

'A' CHRISTMAS COLLECTION
Harold Kempka

Jeremy spotted the tables of knick-knacks on the front lawn of a dilapidated old house and pulled over. After spending the morning perusing garage sales anyway, he figured one more wouldn't hurt.

He loved the rush of excitement in finding a rare piece of memorabilia someone considered an outdated piece of junk. He'd haggle, get it for next to nothing, and then sell it for a nice profit, capitalizing on other people's stupidity.

Jeremy found a box of hand-blown Christmas ornaments that appeared hand-painted on the inside in the style of Currier and Ives, and perhaps dated back to the late 1800's. He picked it up, and breathed the Christmassy, outdoors aroma of pine needles emanating from it.

The decorations appeared to be in good condition, except for their lost luster. Paint cracks marred the detailed images of people on sleigh rides or sitting hearthside staring outward at the ornament glass.

His hands trembled as he carefully examined each of the fragile glass orbs. The last one's highly reflective surface made it look nearly new, and not part of the set. A faint image on the inside that resembled a countryside scene of new fallen snow illuminated by a full moon, made it look like it was an unfinished piece.

"May I help you?" A gravelly voice from behind said.

"Uh, yeah," he said, nearly dropping the ornament.

He spun around to find a hunched over, wafer thin old woman, brow furrowed and head cocked to one side staring up at him.

"How much do you want for this mismatched set of old ornaments?"

"Why would you want those old things?" she asked, waving her hand. "You can buy new ones for about the same amount of money."

114

"I know, but there's a nostalgic feeling about them," he replied, fighting back a broad smile that said he was about to screw her out of them.

She wrinkled her blood-vessel road mapped nose. "How about twenty dollars?"

"Are you serious, lady?" he said. "Look at the paint cracks, and how faded they are. Besides, they're not even a complete set."

"You trying to take advantage of an old lady?"

"No ma'am. They remind me of some ornaments my grandparents put on their tree when I was a kid," he said. "I really loved Christmas at their house. I'll give you five bucks. That's a buck apiece, and I'll even take the one that doesn't match the others."

She studied him for several seconds. "Well, it sounds like you want to relive better times. Tell you what, give me ten dollars, and it's a deal."

"Great," he said.

Jeremy hurried home, and checked the ornaments on numerous websites, but found nothing that even resembled them.

After awhile he felt tingly, like his arms and legs had fallen asleep. Jeremy stepped away from the computer and walked around to get the circulation going. Then, he poured himself a glass of wine and sat in his easy chair with the box of ornaments.

Jeremy re-examined each one until his eyes burned and the ornaments' images appeared blurry. The tolling Westminster chimes on the grandfather clock told him it was late.

He gulped the remaining wine in his glass, and rested his head against the back of the chair. As he rubbed his tired eyes, little specs of light flashed behind his eyelids.

A few hours later he awakened, shivering uncontrollably. He stood alongside a country road, ankle-deep in freshly fallen snow, wearing Victorian-style winter clothing. It was nighttime and although there was no moon or stars, a silver sheen illuminated the wintery landscape.

He heard some bells jingling and the "clop, clop, clop" of a horse. Jeremy waved frantically and tried to run toward a couple approaching in a horse-drawn sleigh.

"Help me, please!" he yelled, but his feet were stuck to the ground.

The couple drove by, smiling and cuddling up to each other. They ignored him as though he didn't exist.

The old woman stepped from the shadows in Jeremy's living room. She held the glass ornament up to the light.

"Ah, my collection is finally complete," she said, admiring the silvery image of a man standing alongside a road waving to a horse-drawn sleigh.

She set the ornament in the box and closed the cover. Jeremy stood alongside the road screaming helplessly as a shroud of sudden darkness swallowed him up.

LIL' GIGGLES

Stephanie Kincaid

Jessie didn't tell her parents that the doll frightened her. She didn't want to seem like a cowardly little baby. She even worked the doll into her toy rotation, playing with it dutifully, then putting it away with relief. This was less for her parents' benefit than for the doll's. Jessie feared that if she didn't play with the thing enough, it might become angry with her, and she didn't want to think about the possible consequences of the creepy doll's anger.

The doll had come with its own name—Lil' Giggles— and it was supposed to laugh when you squeezed it. Mercifully, the noisemaking mechanism had broken in shipping, so Jessie never had to hear the creepy doll giggle. Still, its lips were frozen open, its little rounded teeth bared in an eerie parody of mirth. The thing sported a sculpted tuft of bright red hair that was set back just a little too far on its high bulbous forehead. Its dull black eyes were unnaturally wide, and they rolled when Jessie moved the doll so that no matter how she held it, Lil' Giggles always seemed to be staring at her.

She had tried setting the doll down so that it faced away from her, but she couldn't stop stealing glances at it, fearing that its oversized head would turn itself around so those dead eyes could find her again.

The longer the doll lived in Jessie's room among her lovable and nonthreatening bunnies and bears, the stronger Jessie's fear grew. After a while, she found herself checking the cabinet under the bathroom sink before she used the toilet just to make sure Lil' Giggles hadn't concealed itself among the towels, waiting for a vulnerable moment.

She engaged in lengthy staring contests with the doll, her eyes watering as she fought to keep from blinking, certain that during the fraction of a second that her eyes were closed, the doll would move.

It was during one of these tests of Jessie's will that she learned the true depth of ultimate horror. She was supposed to be trying to sleep, but she had unthinkingly left Lil' Giggles too near the night light, and the blue glow lent the doll's usual pallor a deathly cast. Jessie stared at it from across the room. She felt sure that if she closed her eyes for so much as an instant, she'd feel a cold little hand touch her, and as soon as she looked, she'd see that the silently laughing doll had abandoned its seat near the night light and crawled into bed with her and...

"Eee-hee-hee-hee! Eee-hee-hee-hee!" A high-pitched cackle shattered Jessie's thoughts. She screamed. It had happened! Lil' Giggles had come to life and was cackling maniacally over and over again. Any moment now, it would move toward her. She prayed that Mommy and Daddy would rescue her before the doll could get her.

The maniacal giggles continued. Jessie shrank back into the bed. It was just the opportunity for which the advancing teddy bear had been waiting. Its tiny fangs tore into the back of her neck. Powerless to help its owner, Lil' Giggles did the only thing it could: it kept up its shrill alarm. Jessie hadn't heeded its warning, but perhaps her parents would come before it was too late.

Contributors

Dawn Allison lives in the backwaters of North Carolina where her closest neighbors are two abandoned pig farms that creak in the night. You can check out her work in *Necrotic Tissue*, *Burst* literary e-zine, *Bards and Sages Quarterly*, and others. The complete list is here: huntingthemidnightmuse.wordpress.com/published

Kent Alyn is a Seattle-based fiction writer, husband, and father of three. Just like his website, kentalyn.com, he's a continual work in progress.

Alan Baxter is an author living on the south coast of NSW, Australia. He writes dark fantasy, sci fi and horror, rides a motorcycle and loves his dog. He also teaches Kung Fu. Read extracts from his novels, a novella and short stories at his website—www.alanbaxteronline.com—and feel free to tell him what you think. About anything.

Adam Blomquist was raised on a steady diet of candy corn, rock 'n roll, classic literature and horror movies. This mix severely warped his brain. He currently attends Boston University where he studies English and Film. You can find his blog and more of his work at www.brain-tremors.com and in the pages of *Shroud Magazine* issue #7.

John Boden resides in the shadow of Three Mile Island with his wonderful wife and children. He is an editor for *Shock Totem* magazine.

L.R. Bonehill never meant to hurt anyone all those years ago; he just wanted to play, that's all. Forgive him online at http://bonehillsboneyard.blogspot.com

AJ Brown rarely takes himself seriously, but when he does, he pens stories from the tears of women he's never met. You can find him here, there and not quite everywhere, but mostly at his web blog, Type AJ Negative at: http://typeajnegative.wordpress.com/

Jameson T. Caine has at one time or another worked as a carpenter, meat cutter, shipping clerk, forklift operator, assembly line worker, long haul truck driver and minister. Currently he drives a tanker truck by day and calls himself a writer by night, the latter fueled by a steady diet of soda and salty snacks. He has numerous stories appearing online and in print. He lives in Northern California with his wife and two dogs. Visit him online at http://jamesontcaine.blogspot.com/

Brendan David Carson is a writer of science fiction, fantasy and horror. He has been published in *Aurealis*, *Year's Best Australian Science Fiction* and a number of other magazines. His blog is at brendandcarsonsfiction.blogspot.com, he went to Clarion South 2009 and he is facebookable.

Brad Chacos is a business writer whose fiction has appeared in several publications, including *Necrotic Tissue*, *Withersin*, and the final issue of *Nossa Morte*. Neighbors say he's a decent enough fellow.

Michael Colangelo is a writer from Toronto. Visit him at michaelrcolangelo.blogspot.com

Nick Contor was born in 1968, which explains all the protests. He has managed to survive thus far and writes things down occasionally in southern New Mexico, pausing now and again to eat, sleep and enjoy life with his wife and two children. This is his first published story.

Alan W. Davidson is employed as a structural steel draftsman and lives, with his wife and son, on the continent's edge in the old city of St. John's. He is a member of the Writer's Alliance of Newfoundland and Labrador and is taking baby steps towards writing his first novel. You are invited to attend his ramblings at http://conversationsfromlandsedge.blogspot.com

Scott Davis ran out of books worth reading at his town library north of Boston, so started writing late in 2007. He has been published ten times since. He imagines that it will be easier to change people to suit a colony planet than terraform it. How far can you stray from the human genome though, before you create a monster? He keeps his readers informed at: universeofpossibilities.blogspot.com

Laura Eno lives in Florida with a very tolerant husband, three skulking cats and an absurdly happy dog. She has a pet from the Underworld named Jezebel and a skull called Mr. Fluffy who help her write novels late at night. Please visit her strange imagination at http://lauraeno.blogspot.com

Danielle Ferries lives in Brisbane, Queensland (Australia) and adores dark and dreary weather, wicked characters with fractured worlds, gothic horror, collecting creepy dolls and Hitchcock. Other publications include stories with *Darkened Horizons*, *Black Hound* (Atrum Tempestas Anthology), *Sinister Tales*, *Flashes in the Dark*, and the *Festive Fear Anthology* with Tasmaniac Publications.

Cate Gardner's stories have appeared in *Fantasy Magazine*, *Postscripts*, and *Shock Totem*. Her short fiction collection, *Strange Men in Pinstripe Suits*, published by Strange Publications, is available, and her novella, *Theatre of Curious Acts* will be published by Hadley Rille Books in 2011.

Christopher Green was born in the United States. After moving to Australia at the age of 20, he attended Clarion South and has been published in *Dreaming Again, Beneath Ceaseless Skies*, and *Abyss &Apex*. His work has been nominated for an Australian Shadows Award and several Aurealis Awards. When he isn't writing, he's thinking about writing, unless he's talking to his wife, at which point he is most certainly listening to what she has to say. Honest. He maintains a blog at christophergreen.wordpress.com

Rachel Green is a forty-something writer from Derbyshire, England. She lives with her two partners and three dogs. Her novel *An Ungodly Child* was published in 2008 and *Screaming Yellow* in 2010. She also writes poetry, paints and illustrates. When not writing, Rachel walks her three dogs, potters in the garden, drinks copious amounts of tea and stabs people with swords. www.leatherdyke.co.uk is a portal site to her photograph and fiction blogs. She can also be found on Facebook (Rachel Green) and posts daily haiku on Twitter (@leatherdykeuk)

Uri Grey is a game writer, translator, humanist, twitterist and storyteller from Israel. His work has been published in numerous magazines and anthologies. He lives in urigrey.com and rather enjoys the view.

Harper Hull was born and raised in Northern England and now lives in South Carolina with his Dixie wife and 4 vicious dogs. He started writing fiction in 2009 after doing it corporately for too long and has a delightful cross-section of work scheduled to appear in 2010 with hopefully more to come. His favorite authors are Ballard, Bradbury, Tartt and McCarthy. You can track Harper online at http://harperhull.weebly.com/

Jeremy Kelly is deathly afraid of people. Visit him and some of his other stories over at jointhebirdies.blogspot.com , but don't expect him to do the talking and be prepared for uncomfortable silences.

Harold 'Hal' Kempka is a former Marine and Vietnam Veteran. His short stories have been published in *Dark Valentine, Thrillers Killers and Chillers, Night to Dawn, Golden Visions, House of Horror UK, 69 Flavors of Paranoia, Night to Dawn, Blood Moon Rising, The New Flesh, Sex and Murder,* and *Death Head Grin,* among others. Hal also has stories appearing in upcoming anthologies from Pill Hill Press and Blood Bound Books. He is a member of the FlashXer flash fiction workshop, and lives in Southern California. His email address is: rvnvet6667@yahoo.com

Stephanie Kincaid is a freelance editor and writer who lives in Oklahoma. She has an MA in literature and a weakness for bad horror movies. She highly recommends being very, very nice to your toys.

Daniel LeMoal lives and writes in Winnipeg, Manitoba, Canada. His work has previously appeared in *On Spec, Apex Science Fiction & Horror Digest* and Ellen Datlow's *Best Horror of the Year* anthology.

Ken Muise has been an active-duty Soldier for 15 years. His stories have appeared or are forthcoming in *Flashes in the Dark, The Nautilus Engine, Hypersonic Tales, Full of Crow* and the *Horror House.* He blogs at www.elmuise.blogspot.com. When he isn't reading, writing or working he enjoys terrorizing his three daughters via Facebook.

Doug Murano lives somewhere in the wide-open spaces of the Great Plains. When he's not at his day job, he composes dark little stories and is an associate editor for *Necrotic Tissue* magazine. Visit him online at http://muranofiction.blogspot.com

Joe L. Murr has lived on every continent except Antarctica. He currently divides his time between Finland and the Netherlands. His fiction has been published or is forthcoming in *Dark Recesses, Necrotic Tissue, Read by Dawn I & II*, and other publications. Visit him online at joelmurr.blogspot.com

Brendan P. Myers stories have appeared in such publications as the *Northern Haunts* anthology from Shroud Publishing and *Malpractice: An Anthology of Bedside Terror* from Stygian Publications. He can be found online at http://bpmyers.blogspot.com

Barry Napier has had over 30 short stories and poems published in print and online. HIs short fiction has been collected in *Debris,* and his chapbook *The Final Study of Cooper M. Reid* is available through Strange Publications. His most recent release is a book of poetry titled *A Mouth for Picket Fences,* available through Needfire Press. Keep up with his masochistic writing habits at www.barrynapierwriting.wordpress.com

Joe Nazare has sold fiction and poetry to such markets as *Shroud, Pseudopod, Damnation Books, Death in Common,* and *Vicious Verses and Reanimated Rhymes.* He also writes the daily blog Macabre Republic (www.macabre-republic.com).

Brad Nelson is a former backyard samurai and blue jeans Zen master who spends most of his time now on the back porch with his pipe and a cup of coffee. He retired his sword and took up the pen after serving five years as an interrogator in the U.S. Army. Brad is also a creative writing M.F.A. candidate at National University and Chief Editor of *Eclectic Flash,* a new online literary journal. You can find *Eclectic Flash* at www.eclecticflash.com. Brad's literary endeavors are forthcoming from a number of online and print publications—just as soon as he can decide where to send each piece.

Kurt Newton lives as a recluse in the woods of northeast Connecticut. He has been spotted on his plot of land harvesting grubs from rotted logs, setting tripwires for small animals and drinking from fresh water streams. He uses wood pulp and dried viscera to make the paper on which he writes his stories. He drives a black Ford Focus.

John Paolicelli is a 48 year old new writer that lives on Long Island NY with his wife and five Ridgebacks. This charming sociopath works as a manufacturing manager by day and a breeder of champion Rhodesian Ridgebacks by night. When not cleaning up puppy crap, he attempts to write and watch TV. He is an active member of the Science Fiction Writers Workshop.

Jonathan Pinnock has had over 100 short stories and poems published in places both exalted and downright unsalubrious. He has even won a prize or two and had work broadcast on BBC Radio 4. His novel *Mrs Darcy vs. The Aliens* will be published by Proxima in Summer 2011. He is married with two slightly grown-up children and he blogs at http://www.jonathanpinnock.com

Joshua Rainey lives in WA with his wife Delores and kids Billy, Dream, Sophia, and Aidan. He also has 3 cats Bronson, Cherry Darling, and Gumball. His short story Scotch on Rocks was published in *Black Petals* #42.

Chris Reed is the author of more than 50 short stories. His fiction has appeared in a variety of small press publications including *Black Ink Horror*, *Chimeraworld 5*, and the Cutting Block Press anthology, *Tattered Souls: The Provocative Boundary of Fear*. Aside from writing, he enjoys frozen pizza, Seinfeld reruns, and hockey fights. He lives in Davison, MI, with his photographer wife and their two enigmatic children. Visit his official Web site: www.ChrisReedFiction.com.

Patrick Rutigliano resides in Indiana with his wife, Hannah, and a cat possessing the power of mesmerism. Residing online at patrickrutigliano.blogspot.com, his first collection of short stories, *Black Corners of a Blood-Red Room*, is now available from Library of Horror Press.

C. L. Scarr currently lives in Cincinnati, Ohio, penning short fiction across a wide variety of genres, and is also a freelance editor with credits such as the wildly popular Secret Service Agent series by Stephen Templin and *Dark Pages Volume 1* from Blade Red Press.

Karen Schindler writes even when she's not writing. A wonderer, a cherisher of life and experiences, she lives life with gleeful abandon and pulls others into her wake. Karen has been or is about to be published at *Eclectic Flash*, *Voxpoetica*, *WeirdYear*, *52 Stitches*, *Flashes in the Dark*, *InkNode*, *Negative Suck* and various other ezines and print anthologies. You can find more of her work at *Miscellaneous Yammering*.

Canadian fiction writer, poet, and playwright **J. J. Steinfeld** lives on Prince Edward Island. He has published fourteen books—ten short story collections, two novels, two poetry collections—the most recent ones being *Word Burials* (Novel, Crossing Chaos Enigmatic Ink, 2009), *Misshapenness* (Poetry, Ekstasis Editions, 2009), and *A Glass Shard and Memory* (Stories, Recliner Books, 2010). His short stories and poems have appeared in numerous anthologies and periodicals internationally, and over forty of his one-act plays and a handful of full-length plays have been performed in Canada and the United States.

Mike Stone was born in 1966 in Stoke-on-Trent, England. Since losing most of his eyesight he has retreated from your world to travel the dark corners of inner space—or to put it more prosaically he thinks "What if?" a lot. The signs are clear to those that know him well, for his one not-so-bad eye glazes over and he is rendered deaf to all English except for "Would you like a cup of tea, Mike?" He will then engage with reality long enough to ask if there are any biscuits before drifting off again. He supposes this can be very trying for those around him, but remains unrepentant. 2011 will see the publication of his novella, *Lemon Man*, and a collection of short stories, called *Memory Bones*. His vanity has a name: www.mylefteye.net

Samuel Montgomery-Blinn is a software engineer by trade who lives, works, and writes in Durham, North Carolina with his wife, two kids, and three cats. The cats help out as they can with his newest vocation as editor and publisher of a quarterly magazine of speculative fiction, *BULL SPEC*, at bullspec.com.

Anna Taborska was born in London, England. She is an award-winning filmmaker and writer of horror stories, screenplays and poetry. Her stories and poems have been published in a number of anthologies, including *And Now the Nightmare Begins: THE HORROR ZINE* (2009), *The Black Book of Horror* volumes 5, 6 and 7 (2009-2010), *Christmas: Peace on All The Earths* (2010) and *No Fresh Cut Flowers, An Afterlife Anthology* (2010). Anna's short story "Bagpuss" was a finalist for the Eric Hoffer Award and is now published in *Best New Writing 2011*.

While living in a sun drenched country is nice, **Brenton Tomlinson** finds his mind continually delves into places that are not so warm and comforting. Strangely he seems to enjoy this. Writing credits include:52

Stitches 2009, *Fear and Trembling*, and *Yellow Mama*. New work will be published in: *The Blackness Within* anthology from Apex and *Night to Dawn* magazine. He is the editor for Blade Red Press *Dark Pages Volume 1* anthology. And for something different, he is currently working on a YA novel. For more information you can read his blog at musingsofanaussiewriter.blogspot.com

Jim Valenti is a professional engineer fixing the many large suspension bridges in New York City by day, and a married father of three dealing with the numbing reality of middle-age by night. Jim views life as he thinks it should be—rife with weird opportunities around every corner. He never passes up the challenge of a good wiffleball game.

After a twenty year period of procrastination **Deborah Walker** has started to write short stories and poetry. She lives in London with her partner Chris and her two lovely, yet distracting young children. Find her stories in *Nature's Futures*, *Cosmos*, and *Through the Eyes of the Undead*.

K. Allen Wood lives and plots in Massachusetts. A former musician and music journalist, he began the transition into fiction two years ago. For more info, visit his website at http://www.kallenwood.com.

Mercedes M. Yardley writes about beauty and horror. They are more intertwined than you might think. Visit her blog at www.abrokenlaptop.wordpress.com.

Jamie Eyberg
(1974-2010)

Jamie was a good writer and friend, but most of all a great and kind man. We shared stories and novels, helped critique each other's work, and cheered each victory in this ruthless game. His short stories appeared in over two-dozen publications, including *M-Brane Science Fiction*, *Midnight Echo*, and *Fissure Magazine*.

Those of us who write sometimes live in strange, insular bubbles. The internet has made contact between bubbles easier.

I am glad to have known you, Jamie.

Made in the USA
Charleston, SC
14 December 2010